To Joline,

A Star Rises
in
Persia

A NOVEL

Enjoy,

Floss Craig

A Star Rises in Persia

A NOVEL

FLOSS CRAIG

A STAR RISES IN PERSIA
Copyright © 2007 Floss Craig

ISBN 978-1-886068-08-7
Library of Congress Control Number: 2007922316

Fiction · Religious and Inspirational · Faith

Published by Fruitbearer Publishing
P.O. Box 777, Georgetown, DE 19947
(302) 856-6649 · FAX (302) 856-7742
www.fruitbearer.com

Graphic design by Candy Abbott
Edited by Muriel Webb
Cover photo of Tamar Hennessy by Joy Craig
Interior illustratration by Cynthia Hale

Printed in the United States of America

DEDICATED TO

Joy

Michael

Elizabeth

Nate

Dan

Stephen

Rebecca

Chapter 1

"OVER HERE, YOUNG LADIES!" THE SHOPKEEPER CALLED.

Tavita and I turned toward the hefty, bearded man who stood by a cart piled high with fruit and vegetables. We came to the market in Susa several times a week now that we were old enough to shop for our families. Raising my voice over the din of animals braying and neighing, and people calling to each other up and down the street, I said to Tavi, "Let's see if we can outwit him today."

"My mother says we can't outsmart him, but he will let us think we have. We have only been shopping for a short time and he's been selling for fifty years."

People from all over the world traveled to this city and to this bazaar. We were as buzzing bees bringing back reports each day to Tavi's mother about something new we saw there. And we always saw something new.

Bur burrr! Bur burrr!

Tavi and I jumped at the shrill sound of trumpets and fell backwards into what had been a neatly piled basket of ripe, red mangoes.

"My fruit! My fruit!" the sun-shriveled old shopkeeper yelled as he scrambled on his knees to retrieve his produce before the pressing crowd squashed them into the cobbled street.

"My gorgeous mangoes!" he growled. "What have you done?"

As I tried to get up, my hands scattered them even more.

"I'm sorry," I rasped, though I'm sure he didn't hear me.

"Esther," said Tavi as she rose to her feet, "Are you all right?"

The trumpet blasts had startled the donkeys and camels, and their braying added to the chaos. People squeezed together as the crowd parted from the road, revealing three heralds in tunics of crimson, yellow and blue, multi-colored streamers flowing from their glistening, gold trumpets, raised for another blast.

"Make way! Make way! Bow before Her Highness Queen Vashti!" ordered a herald. "Bow before Her Highness Queen Vashti! Clear the way!"

Stomp, stomp, stomp, stomp. The sound of marching soldiers drowned all of the other noises as the waves of shoppers continued to separate like the Red Sea parting for Moses. Men, women and children knelt with their heads bowed. My heart raced wildly as I lowered myself to the ground and craned my neck.

"I want to see her." I whispered desperately to Tavi.

She grabbed my arm. "Over here."

Tall grain baskets were stacked beside a booth. We scurried behind them and squatted down where we could peek through to watch the procession. It seemed like lightning flashing as the sun struck the soldiers' shields.

"There!" I sprung from my hiding place, but Tavi grabbed my outstretched arm and pulled me back down. Several people turned with disapproval in our direction. My heart pounded so hard that I covered my chest with both hands and held my breath. The queen's carriage approached. It had a cover of embroidered tapestry with gold tassels that swayed as it moved. And the horses! I had never seen such regal steeds with their tails and manes braided and adorned with ribbons. Their bridles blazed with medallions bearing the royal insignia.

I gasped so loud that Tavi put her hand over my mouth. "Esther, quiet."

I had never been so excited in my life. There she was—Queen Vashti of Persia. A thin veil covered most of her face, but her onyx eyes sparkled as they glanced over the crowds. Jeweled ornaments across her forehead shone like tiny stars. Her silk gown glimmered in shades of amethyst, catching reflections from the sun like bits of crystal.

After I settled down and my heart stopped pounding in my ears, Tavi and I crept from behind the baskets. Then we hid behind booths as we followed the carriage. As though I were hypnotized, I could not keep my eyes off the queen. For an instant, it seemed that the queen looked directly at me. We did not know it then, but that was the last day Vashti would be honored as queen of this great empire.

We watched until her carriage outdistanced us on its way to the Citadel. Its walls stood high above all the other buildings in Susa. No matter where a person was in the city, the king's center of government was visible. The stables housed more than a thousand horses. King Ahasuerus' army was a formidable enemy and no one imagined that any conquering army could penetrate the thick, high walls of his Citadel.

I thought that thousands of soldiers must have marched by us that day. Some led wagons with gold, silver and bronze treasures piled high.

"I wonder if those treasures have been looted from another country," I said to Tavi. A shiver ran through me as I wondered if there had been a celebration like that when the Persian army conquered my Jewish nation four generations earlier. My stomach tightened and my teeth clenched at the thought of soldiers killing and rampaging through a town. I shook my head to rid myself of that horror.

As the dust settled on the road, Tavi said, "I wonder what it would be like to live in a palace. I think that the queen would have at least a dozen maids just waiting to do whatever she commanded."

"She wouldn't have to buy food at the bazaar as we do," I said. "And I'm sure she doesn't have to cook or scrub floors either."

"Or wash her own clothes," Tavi said.

"Maybe all she has to do," I said as I combed my hair with my fingers, "is to look beautiful for the king. I suppose it would be nice for a while, but I would miss coming to the bazaar and watching everyone. It's fun, don't you think, Tavi?"

She agreed. Continuing our walk through the bazaar, I made up a poem as I often did.

"I feel the muse coming on me, Tavi."

"I'm ready. Let me hear it," she said.

"Clothes in rainbow colors
Skin of every hue

Mint and saffron mingle
Pleasant milieu

"Anise for the rice dish
Spicy cardamom and curry
Walnuts, onions, pomegranates
Pecans and mulberries

"Daily to the market
For linens, silk and gold
Donkeys pulling wagons
Merchandise bought and sold."

"Esther," Tavi said, "You've forgotten to include a part about the queen and the soldiers that we saw today."

I smiled, tipped my head and closed my eyes.

"Soldiers march in unison
Heralds blast their horns
The lovely queen floats on a cloud
Drawn by a dozen unicorns."

"Unicorns?" said Tavi.

"Why not? A dozen horses wouldn't sound poetic."

"Or how about 'prancing steeds'?"

I smiled at her. "Yes, I like that. I'll consider it."

We came upon our favorite booth in the bazaar. The awning was royal blue with yellow tassels. On a table covered with black velvet, the shopkeepers displayed jewelry and decorative hair ornaments. We sat on stools at the table, took our hair and piled it on top of our heads, braiding and tucking it this way and that. Mehira and her husband Aziz were the shopkeepers. Although quite old, Mehira always dressed as though she were going to a wedding. Today she wore a flowing, emerald green gown. She had a ring on every finger and long earrings dangled with what looked like precious gems. It was difficult to tell if they were real or fake.

She looked at Tavi and me sideways. "You girls always look, but never buy. Perhaps you should stop your daydreaming and make room for real customers. Don't you have chores to do? Have you even started your marketing?"

Tavi looked down at our baskets sitting on the ground beside us. "Esther, our baskets are still empty. We haven't gotten anything yet."

We both shared a hearty laugh. "We've gotten sidetracked this morning. Let's hurry."

"Goodbye Mehira," we said as we hopped off the stools. Gathering my skirt around me in my haste, I tripped as my feet touched the ground.

Mehira shook her head and waved a hand at me. "You are too clumsy to be a fine lady, Esther. Go home and do your work before the day grows too hot!"

Tavi and I grabbed our baskets and hurried toward a vegetable stand. "It's already too hot. A lizard would fry on the street," I said.

"Freshest fruit in all the market! Over here, ladies," a merchant yelled to our neighbors Dinah and Eliza whose baskets were nearly full. "You won't find anything better than my pomegranates and mangos."

"Who are you kidding, Round One?" Dinah said, "You can brag all you want, but everyone knows that your produce is left over from last week! Ha, ha, ha!"

Shaking his finger at her, the man hollered, "Oh, if you were not a woman . . . Turning his back to Dinah, he began to rearrange his fruit, but Dinah was not finished.

"If I were a man, you wouldn't try to cheat me."

She walked away. Dinah must have been pleased with her pithy comeback. I knew she enjoyed bantering with Persian vendors because a Jewish man would never speak to her in public that way.

Tavi and I finished our shopping after purchasing mangoes, figs, almonds, flour and cinnamon raisin cakes that smelled wonderful. When we returned to her house, we burst in the door.

"Mother, you won't believe who we saw today."

"The queen!" I blurted. "Queen Vashti!"

"She was so pretty."

"More than pretty!" I said. "Beautiful! She is amazing, more than any other person in the whole world!"

"And the horses were decorated, too."

"Yes! The horses had jeweled medallions on their heads and bridles."

"She had a million guards and there were heralds blowing trumpets! You should have seen her, Mother."

Aunt Mehry smiled as she listened, and then wiped her floured hands on her apron. She was not my real aunt, but as a close neighbor of Mordecai and friend of my deceased parents, she had helped look after me as long as I could remember. I sometimes called her "Momma."

"The procession is part of a festival by King Ahasuerus," she said. "He's planning an attack on Greece, and he is so confident of his victory that he's celebrating before he even goes to battle." With her hands on her hips, she shook her head. "A war not yet begun and a victory not yet won."

Tavi's little brother Micah had stopped playing and looked up from the floor wide-eyed. For a change, he had nothing to say.

"Why do they celebrate before the war begins, Momma?" Tavita said. "Suppose they lose the battle?"

Aunt Mehry folded her arms across her chest. "The king probably never considered that possibility. He must instill confidence in his men, and defeat is not an option." Turning her attention to me, she said, "Now, you'd better be getting home, Esther. Mordecai was looking for you earlier. You were gone a lot longer than usual today."

I tousled little Micah's hair and kissed Tavi's mother on the cheek.

"I'll see you later, Tavi!" I called as I hurried into the street.

My cousin, Mordecai, had been raising me since the death of my parents when I was young, and I loved him like a father. When I came through the door into our home, Mordecai looked up from the scroll he was reading. People said he was a handsome man, thirty years older than I, but he never married.

He dressed in a colorful tunic because he often spent the day at the palace gate and brought news to our community of all that was happening throughout the empire.

"There you are," he said. "You and Tavita took a long time this morning at the bazaar. Did you get caught up in all the excitement?"

"Yes! It was thrilling to see Queen Vashti. She's as beautiful as everyone says."

"I suppose she is, Esther. The king would not have it any other way. It is one way he says to the world that he not only is the greatest monarch in the world, but also has the very best of all that the world can offer—including the most beautiful woman. Of course, you will give the queen competition when you've grown up." He laughed. "Enough about the queen. I have something special for you."

"Really? What is it?"

Cousin snatched up a package from the table. His eyes sparkled as he handed it to me.

I fumbled with the red cord. "What is this? A gift? But today isn't a special day, is it?"

Dropping the cord onto the floor, I unraveled the covering. It was a scroll with intricately carved rods resembling flames on each end. They were inlaid with gold, giving the illusion that by touching them, I would burn my hands. I looked up at Cousin Mordecai who nodded, his lips pressed tightly. Slowly, I opened the scroll to see what was written inside, half expecting to see the characters written in gold ink. There was no writing. I ran my fingertips over the parchment's soft, uneven ripples.

"This is wonderful, but why are you giving me such an elaborate scroll? It seems like something to be found in a noble home or in a temple."

He bowed ceremoniously and said, "My lady, it is for you to record your poetry, thoughts and the important events in your life, just as the scribes do for the king."

"But I'm not a prophet, a princess, or anyone special. I'm just . . . just an ordinary girl." Many noble Persian women were educated, but few foreigners, including the Jews, were literate. Our responsibilities were in the home.

"There is nothing ordinary about you, Esther." He put his hands on my shoulders. "It's not every girl who knows her people's history, and how to read and write. Do you think I spent time teaching you for nothing?" He smiled widely. "Besides, just as your name means 'Star,' your life will be one that shines as a star in a dark world."

"You exaggerate, my dear cousin, but I enjoy your flattery. Thank you so much. The scroll is wonderful. I can't wait to begin recording "The Chronicles of Esther.""

I curtsied, then hugged him tightly around the neck.

Dear Judah,

The name I have chosen for my chronicles is "Judah," my homeland. I have never been there, but my ancestors told many stories about our country before the captivity and their journeys to Jerusalem to worship at Solomon's temple. They said it was a hard but good life. We have heard that in Judah, even today, the dirt roads are rough and people must wash their clothes in a river. I'm glad that here in Susa there is water irrigation, and it is against the law to pollute the river with washing. In addition, the king's road runs across the empire with highways between large cities like Susa and Persepolis. Life is good here, but I often wonder what it would have been like to live in my own country. I would like to go there someday . . . with my husband.

My husband . . . I haven't thought much about this before, but now, since I am eleven years old, it is time for us to think about my betrothal. I will become a woman soon and will be starting a new season of life.

I woke up the next morning to the sound of anxious voices in the street. Pulling my dress over my head and slipping into my sandals, I dashed into the front room and noticed that Cousin was already outside talking with the neighbors. He wore his turban, indicating that he had already done official business that day. Calling from the doorway, I asked, "What's wrong? What's going on, Cousin Mordecai?"

"Good morning, Esther—just a lot of gossip about something that happened at the Citadel last night."

"It must be important to have the whole neighborhood buzzing like this."

"The women will fill you in as you walk to the bazaar this morning. They're better at telling stories than I am."

Too excited to eat, I grabbed my basket and ran over to Tavi's house.

"Will your mother tell me what's going on, Tavi?"

Tavi looked up from the table while she munched on freshly baked bread.

"Good morning, Esther. You're up early. Have you eaten?" Aunt Mehry said, handing me a piece of bulgur bread sprinkled with cinnamon.

"Who can sleep with all that noise?" I reached for the bread. "Thank you."

Aunt Mehry patted my arm. "Come. We'll walk with the neighbors to the market and see what we can discover about what happened last night at the Citadel." She picked up a basket and headed to the door. Several women huddled close together, moving in the direction of the bazaar. Tavi and I squeezed right into the middle of them.

Mehira and Dinah's faces flushed as they told everyone what they had heard.

"Last night at his banquet, King Ahasuerus wanted to show everyone how beautiful Queen Vashti was," said Dinah. "He ordered her to come in her royal robe and crown, but the queen refused to go."

Some gasped and covered their mouths with their hands. Someone clucked her tongue, and others shook their heads.

"But why?" someone asked. "Why would the queen refuse? It would be an honor."

"No one knows why, except the queen, I suppose. Perhaps it was because she thought the men were drunk; after all, the feasting has gone on for seven days."

Mehira said, "The queen was having her own party with the women and may not have wanted to be disturbed. On the other hand, it could have been very late and she was already asleep. That's probably it. You know how men can be." She snickered and got a nod of agreement from Dinah.

"Perhaps she, herself, had too much to drink," said another.

"Shush! Remember the girls, please," Aunt Mehry said with her eyes narrowed. I wished she hadn't said that because I wanted to hear everything I could. "Whatever her reason, anyone who wants to live would never refuse a command of the king whether she is a peasant or a queen. She humiliated the king in front of everyone in the empire, and that is inexcusable—even for a queen . . . punishable by death, no doubt."

Heads nodded, brows furrowed, and for a moment, no one spoke.

Finally Dinah spoke in a quieter voice than usual, "I wish all women would stand up to their husbands the way the queen did to hers."

"Perhaps we'd all be dead then," said another.

However, Mehira and some of the older women shook their heads in disagreement.

"No," said Mehira. "The queen must honor the king whatever his request, just as we must honor the king and our husbands."

The atmosphere at the bazaar was different that day—not nearly as crowded, and the voices of vendors were hardly more than a whisper. Tavi and I followed her mother to a booth laden with fabric from all over the world. A place to dream, I thought.

Aunt Mehry unrolled an arms-length of purple silk fabric.

"Nice. How much?" she said to the shopkeeper.

"Twenty taler."

"I'll give you ten."

"I'd rather use it on my mule than give it away for that price."

"Surely an exaggeration," she said. "Why so much? I give you a lot of business. You should give me special rates. I can always go elsewhere, you know."

With his hands on his hips and puffing out his chest, the vendor said, "You come to me because you know I have the best silks and linens in Susa. You want me to go out of business by always meeting your demands for a lower price?"

"You are not the only cloth merchant in Susa. I will see what Moshe has on display this morning. Perhaps he's received a newer shipment."

Aunt Mehry turned and began walking away. She had a slight smile on her face, but not so he could see it.

"You women! Always wanting the best goods for a bargain. You will be the end of me yet! Wait! This one time—the last time I give in to you! You can have it for twelve taler, but do not go around telling your friends that I gave you such a price, or the next time you come here, my stall will be gone. I will be gone. Bankrupt! That's what you do to me!"

He already had the fabric wrapped and put out his hand for the money.

Aunt Mehry put the coins into his palm and smiled. "Good day, sir."

Walking away with her precious bundle, Aunt Mehry said, "Girls, don't let the loud-mouthed vendors scare you off because they expect you to bargain with them. I'm not always as successful as today, but one always has to try."

We nodded respectfully, pleased to be learning the ways of the world. Aunt Mehry also showed Tavi and me how to select the best lamb and fish, examining color, texture and smell.

"The merchants may put yesterday's meat at the front of their stall and wait until that is sold before they display the fresher products. Always ask to see what else they have. Then compare."

We passed a booth where two women sat on the ground weaving a carpet with brilliant colors of red and blue in an intricate pattern. Their hands moved methodically and, it seemed, effortlessly. Some wonderful carpets hung on the wall for display. I stood and admired them until Tavita pulled me away.

Later on, as we sipped mint tea, I told Cousin Mordecai about the argument between Mehira and Dinah, and that Dinah said Queen Vashti was courageous to disobey the king's order and do as she pleased.

"What do you think the king will do about Queen Vashti's behavior, Cousin?"

He said, "It wasn't courage, Esther, but disrespect."

Mordecai stood up from the table and paced a few steps, rubbing his dark brown beard. He sat down again at the table, tipped his chair back and ran his fingers through his thick, curly hair, as if stimulating his thoughts. Then after another sip of tea, he went on.

"Unless the king treats this as a serious offense against his authority, Esther, he will have a lot of trouble throughout the empire when other women follow Vashti's example. She dishonored King Ahasuerus before everyone, and also wronged the princes and all the people. By law, she must be punished. If the king ignores this, he would appear weak, and many others would challenge his authority. That would lead to even greater problems."

Mordecai stood and adjusted his turban. "I must go now to the king's gate and see what new information I can gather. I'll return in time for the evening meal."

"I will see you then, Cousin. I'll prepare the lamb that I purchased this morning . . . at a good price." I flashed him my biggest smile.

"You're growing up, Esther," he said as he walked into the street.

Dear Judah,

It was new to me to think of serious issues and this made my heart heavy. Of course, I had always submitted to Mordecai's authority, and unquestionably I would at the proper time, submit to my husband . . . I believe. However, what if my husband asked me to do something terrible—I don't know what that might be— but suppose he asked me to denounce Jehovah? Could I do that? Should I do that? The law says I must obey my husband, but is his authority greater than Jehovah's? I must speak to Mordecai about this on another day.

During the next few days one topic dominated conversations at the market—Queen Vashti. That was all anyone talked about. Quarrels continued among women in the city who agreed with the queen and those who thought her behavior disrespected the king, making him look like a fool.

"I despise my husband, for he is always ordering me around," said Dinah. "He thinks I'm his slave. I would like to tell him to go to the market himself for his food. Imagine the surprise on his face." She laughed. "HA! And clean his own clothes!"

Another woman added, "Let my husband stay home and care for the children all day. Perhaps he wouldn't think my life is so easy." She waved one hand in the air and snickered. "I would gladly trade places with him so I could spend my days at the harbor watching the ships bringing ivory from Africa, tea and spices from India—"

"And gems from Egypt!" Dinah broke in. She nodded and continued, "That would be far more exciting than my dreary life."

I had never seen my neighbors so upset about anything before. Queen Vashti's example turned friends against one another. I had never before heard the women speak about their feelings openly. I didn't know some of them felt that way about their husbands. I thought they were content with their lives.

Before going our separate ways, Mehira stopped and looked closely at me, as if seeing me for the first time. "Your eyes are magnificent, little girl. Be sure to look down while in the company of men. Once they look into your eyes they will not be able to find their way out."

Mehira's words confused me. I thought everyone's eyes were for seeing, just in different colors. I had heard there were eyes of blue, but I had never seen them. And what did eyes have to do with men?

It was a cloudy, drizzly morning when we learned of the king's pronouncement. A palace herald called out in the Square: "Hear all citizens of Susa! Let it be known that by order of the great King Ahasuerus, Vashti will no longer sit on the throne as queen of Persia. She is banished and will remain in exile for the remainder of her life!"

Though everyone had expected a stern judgment, when it actually happened, shock and sadness filled me. Suppose Vashti had a good reason for denying the king's request, or perhaps she was just too tired to provide entertainment. I sensed that others felt grief also because for the next few days, our walks to the bazaar were quieter than usual. Many women walked with their heads down, avoiding each other's eyes. Cousin Mordecai had been right about the way everyone in the empire would be affected by the queen's action, but we could never have imagined just how much.

Chapter 2

ONE NIGHT I STOOD ON THE ROOFTOP OF MY HOUSE LOOKING UP AT the sky. I contemplated how the same moon and stars that shined down on me here in Persia also shined over the land of Judah. I followed the path of a shooting star, and imagined that I could ride it and see different lands and peoples of the world. I wondered if we would ever go to our own land and worship in Jerusalem for it was a long way from Susa. If we lived there, my Jewish name would be Hadassah.

When I came down from the roof and went inside, I said to Cousin Mordecai, "I've discovered a way to get to Judah and it won't take forever."

"Really, Esther, and how is that?" he asked.

"We'll fly on a shooting star," I told him.

He laughed, but I said, "You'll see."

That night I made a new entry in my chronicles:

"Judah, my Judah
So far away
You still call me your daughter
Though homage I pay
To the Empire of Persia,
Beautiful and bright,
But I long for your borders
On this starry night."

I felt privileged to know how to read and write. Unlike most people that we knew, Cousin Mordecai believed that girls should learn to read and write if they wanted to. In our culture, many people thought that as long as a girl could cook, sew and keep house, that was enough, and some of my friends thought I was foolish to spend time reading and writing, but I disagreed. Cousin Mordecai said that Persia is unlike many parts of the world in that women may be educated and even participate in government affairs. Therefore, for this reason, I am glad we have stayed here— at least for now. Sometimes I recorded psalms of King David who lived about 400 years ago. Mordecai memorized many of them and has taught them to me. This had been a good way to remember my Jewish heritage since it is so different from my life in Susa.

Of course, there are other ways of recording history, like the sculptures of archers and warriors in battle found throughout the city and on the mountainsides. Carvings on cliffs and walls show victorious kings taking captives from foreign lands, although they never record their own defeats.

During a long walk with Cousin one day, I asked him why he became sad whenever we studied the carvings. He pointed to the wall where soldiers with whips walked alongside men bound together like a chain as they walked, their backs stooped.

"This is how our ancestors came to Persia," he said. "The Babylonian armies defeated the Jews, and we were in captivity to them for seventy years in their land. Then the Persians conquered the Babylonians, and many of us were brought here to Persia—the educated ones and artisans. They left only the poor and elderly behind in our homeland."

I felt tears welling up in my eyes. "Did they die there, Cousin?"

He wiped sweat from his brow and the back of his neck, and then cleared his throat before continuing. "I'm sure many of them did, but not all. There was still a remnant left in Judah. Then, about seventy years ago, during the reign of King Cyrus, the king allowed the Jews to leave Persia and return to Jerusalem in order to rebuild Solomon's temple."

"Did he make them go, or could they decide?"

"It was up to every man whether or not to return. Altogether, about 60,000 people went. Many others, like our family, stayed here." He stroked his beard and looked out the window as if visualizing caravans of friends and neighbors starting out on their journey. "I was too young to understand why our family stayed—perhaps it was because life here was easier. This is a land of many cultures; each one bringing the best it has to offer, whether it is in art, science, mathematics or agriculture."

"In Judah," I asked, "was it just Jews, or did others live there also?"

"It was primarily the Jews," he said. "But the nations that conquered us would always leave behind some to maintain their rule."

"Cousin, if you had been older, would you have returned?"

"I would like to think so, Esther, but I cannot be sure. Everything we need to exist in Persia is already established; whereas in Jerusalem, everything had to be rebuilt—even homes to live in since the Babylonians had flattened entire cities. A psalmist wrote about the holy city in a song:

"O God, the nations have come into Your inheritance;
Your holy temple they have defiled;
They have laid Jerusalem in heaps.
The dead bodies of Your servants
They have given as food for the birds of the heavens,
The flesh of Your saints to the beasts of the earth.
Their blood they have shed as water all around Jerusalem,
And there was no one to bury them."

I cried to think of that destruction and became angry. "How could Jehovah allow such a terrible thing? I thought He loved us! Aren't we His chosen ones?"

"He does love us, Esther, but we have rebelled against Him, over and over. We have worshipped other gods, married those who prayed to idols, forgot to teach our children to reverence and obey Him. We have believed we were our own and ignored the wonderful miracles He did for us. We were fools."

"Is that like the punishment you gave me when I lied about sneaking sweets at the market?"

He chuckled. "A little. But yes, that's the idea."

"Then how did some Jews return to Judah if the kings were so cruel to us?"

"Many kings have been used by Jehovah to chasten us, but He gave us favor with King Cyrus who even provided building materials we needed for the work on the temple. The king returned the gold, silver and bronze pieces that originally belonged to the temple treasury."

"So is Solomon's Temple rebuilt now?" I said.

"The altar was rebuilt so that sacrifices could be offered to Jehovah in worship. Unfortunately, very little additional work has been completed because the people of other nationalities continually oppose them. They feared the Jews would become a great nation again, once the city and walls were completed, and then rise up against them."

"Do you think that would happen, Cousin Mordecai?"

He said, "It could. We fought and won many wars trying to conquer all the lands that Jehovah promised to give us: the land of the Canaanites, Hittites, Amorites, Perizzites, Hivites and Jebusites."

I sat up straight, folding my hands in my lap. "Tell me again how Jehovah rescued our people from the Egyptians. That's my favorite story."

"You know it so well, Esther. Why don't you tell me?"

"All right, Cousin Mordecai." I took a deep breath and began. "After Joseph and all his descendants lived in Egypt for a long time, Pharaoh made them slaves. They begged Jehovah to deliver them so he sent Moses, with his brother Aaron, to lead them away. They were running away from Pharaoh's army and had no boats or bridges to cross the Red Sea, so Jehovah sent a strong east wind all night long and made the sea part, leaving bone-dry ground, not even muddy, for the Jews to cross. The best part was when the Egyptian army nearly caught up with them. Then Jehovah made the water close up again, drowning Pharaoh and all his soldiers."

Cousin asked, "When do we remember this deliverance, Esther?"

"When we celebrate Passover."

"Yes," he said. "We are honored to be Jewish."

As wonderful as celebrating Passover was, I enjoyed weddings even more. I wouldn't have admitted that to Cousin Mordecai, but they were so much fun. The last Jewish wedding I attended was of Sheva and Akkub. Sheva was two years older than I was, and the whole community celebrated her wedding to Akkub, the son of Rabbi Addan. We sang, danced, clapped and played musical instruments. Even the oldest people there participated in some way. The men danced together in circles as they held hands, kicked their feet and shouted with laughter.

With all the other girls and women, Tavi and I played on tambourines with long ribbons, waving them in the air, and tapping them in rhythm to the music. It got louder and louder, almost to a frenzy, until with a final furious bang on the tambourines, the music ended.

Exhausted, Tavi and I sat and whispered together about a girl who, the previous year, married a widower who was twenty years older than she was. "She wasn't pretty at all," I said, "and her father had no money for a dowry, so he accepted the first man who made an offer for her since he was afraid no one else would want her. Poor girl."

Tavi shook her head in sympathy and changed the subject.

"Esther, who would you like to marry? Do you have your eye on anyone?"

"Not that it's our choice to make, but I've been noticing Asher, the silversmith's apprentice. I smiled at him a few times when we passed the workshop."

"What did he do?" she said as her eyes widened.

"The first time he turned bright red and quickly turned away, but after that he smiled back. I was embarrassed, but it was fun. What about you, Tavi? I saw Moshe watching you when you got up to dance."

"He did?" Tavi asked clutching my arm.

I nodded and then we both fell quiet for a few moments, perhaps thinking the same thing. One day, we would also stand under canopies next to the men we would spend our lives with, and listen to the rabbi pronounce a blessing on us.

The day following the wedding, Tavi squinted at me and put her forefinger to her temple. "Esther, do you remember Elah dancing yesterday? You know the one with the long, gray beard, and the purple and yellow sash around his waist. His wife died two years ago, and I heard that he is looking for a nice young wife. You would be a perfect match for him. I think I'll have my mother mention it to the matchmaker."

"You will mention it to no one! He is a much better match for you, dear Tavita! Tell your mother," I said, poking her in the chest, "that YOU are interested in Elah!"

The matchmaker in our community was a woman named Jael. I thought that she must have been at least one hundred years old because everywhere she went she bragged about arranging marriages for generations! Tavi said, "That skinny woman Jael looks just like a mountain goat."

When we were younger, Jael once heard us laughing and making goat noises, but Tavi and I ran away and ducked behind some large baskets. It was a good thing that Jael couldn't run as a goat, or she would have caught us and given us a good scolding— and maybe a smack or two!

I wondered if Mordecai would take a wife for himself after I got married. I teased him about this and told him I would ask Jael to find someone for him, but he just smiled.

Finally, the day came when Jael arrived to see Cousin Mordecai. When she knocked, I set down my broom and wiped my hands on my apron, then opened the door.

"Please come in," I said with a quiver in my voice, and showed her to the table where Mordecai waited.

"Esther," said Mordecai, "go next door and see if Tavita's mother needs any help. I'll come for you later."

"Can't I stay? There's work to be done here."

"Esther?"

"Yes, Cousin."

I went outside as slowly as I dared, but he and Jael did not speak until I was out of the house. I knew it was wrong, but I crept around the corner and sat under an open window so I could hear their conversation.

"Mordecai," Jael said. "You know why I am here, so we won't waste time. Your Esther is a pretty girl and will be easy to marry off—providing, of course, that you offer a sufficient dowry. What are you prepared to pay?"

"'Marry off'? We are not discussing a cart full of pomegranates, my dear woman. This is the life of my precious, young cousin. Her future rests in our hands—my hands."

I jumped at the sound of Mordecai's hands slamming the table.

In a quiet voice, he continued. "I will proceed cautiously as I have no experience with these things."

"Yes, of course, my friend," said Jael. "I meant no offense. Please accept my apology, but there are things to discuss, and I will be sensitive, as I always am, with this delicate business."

A huge sigh came from Mordecai. "What is expected? And how long is the process?"

"Formal arrangements need to begin soon because there are many details to attend to, and you don't want the most desirable men to be snatched up while you delay, do you? She should marry in a year or two. Now about the dowry—"

"Just a minute. We have yet to discuss a suitable young man. Esther is a very special girl and not just anyone will do."

At that moment, Tavita walked by and saw me sitting under the window. As she opened her mouth to speak, I waved my arms frantically to warn her to be silent. She looked from me to the window, then stooped and scooted up beside me. The voices inside the house continued.

"Of course not," Jael was saying. "Only the best for your Esther. I have given it considerable thought, and I'm sure you will be pleased with the young man I have in mind. Do you want to know who it is?"

Tavi and I squeezed each other's hands and gritted our teeth.

"Isn't that why you're here, Jael? Who is it then?"

"The wonderful young man I am considering for your Esther is a silversmith's apprentice who will one day have his own shop. He works hard and comes from a good family. A nice family."

Esther realized she hadn't breathed in minutes and took a quick, shallow breath. Silversmith? Asher! She and Tavi's grip on each other tightened.

"And his name . . . ?" said Cousin with much emphasis.

"A wonderful family. Jewish, of course. I know you would want it no other way . . . . All right. His name is Asher. You might know his father, the stonecutter Jehu. His two older sons work with him. Wonderful craftsmen they are."

"Yes. Yes. I know of the family. Not well, but I know of them. A good man, Jehu, I hear."

Jael said, "Yes, of course. Only the best. He is highly respected and I have successfully found good wives for Jehu's two older sons, and now I have in mind your little Esther for his son, Asher."

"Yes, worth consideration. A good match, perhaps." A long pause, then, "I would like to meet with his father Jehu. Then, if I find it agreeable, I will meet Asher, the silversmith."

It was quiet for what seemed to be a long time, so that my pounding heart was the only sound I could hear. Do they know that I'm eavesdropping and are coming to find me? I signaled to Tavi and we crept alongside the house to the corner. We stood and bumped right into her mother!

"Girls! What are you up to?" Aunt Mehry said with a puzzled look.

Neither of us spoke. Aunt Mehry cocked her head, glanced toward the door of my house, then back to us.

"I can guess. Perhaps you two should come inside and give me a hand with cutting vegetables for dinner. Then I can keep my eyes on you."

"Yes ma'm," we said together, and hurried the few steps to her house.

Dear Judah,

A week has passed since Jael and my cousin spoke, and today Jael has brought Asher to our home. When they arrived, I was busy kneading bread. My heart stopped and I bit so hard on my lower lip, I made an indentation. I tried to keep my gaze down, but I stole a few glances—enough to see Asher's soft brown eyes. He caught me looking at him, so I quickly turned my attention to my task until Mordecai told me to go to Aunt Mehry's. There was no hiding under the window this day. I had not wanted to hear their conversation in case it did not go well.

As I went out the door, trying not to make a sound, I heard Jael introducing them and as he greeted Cousin, Asher's voice quavered. Walking quickly to the house next door, I prayed for Mordecai and Asher to come to an agreement.

One afternoon when Tavi's mother was out at the bazaar, Tavi and I went into the workroom where Aunt Mehry had almost finished sewing a bridal gown. We were seldom permitted in the room.

"That gown reminds me of the day we saw Queen Vashti. Wasn't she amazing?" I said as I stroked its silky softness. "Do you think your mother would mind if we tried it on?"

Tavi's brows knit together. She chewed on her thumbnail. "I don't know. I've never asked to try on anything she has made." She came up beside me and then smiled. "Maybe Mother wouldn't notice."

"Right! We will put it back just as we found it. Me first!" I kicked off my sandals. "I'm older and will marry sooner than you."

Tavi put out her hand to stop me. "It's true that you're older, but it's my mother who is making it, so I think I should go first."

Standing straight and stretching my neck, I stuck my nose up in the air and looked down at her through half-closed eyes, and in a deep voice I said, "But I am the queen."

Tavi huffed and put her hands on her hips. "I guess that makes me your maid!"

"Yes, I suppose it does, but afterwards I shall be your maid."

She stood aside and frowned. "Well then, if you insist." As she made an exaggerated curtsy, she said, "Tavita at your service, Your Majesty."

I slipped out of my tunic as Tavi lifted the gown. I will never forget the first time I heard the swishing sound of silk as it swirled over my head and slid over my body. I had never felt so luxurious. The fabric was as light as the touch of a feather. I ran my hands down the flowing skirt to smooth the wrinkles.

"It fits you, Esther—just as if it were made for you. Let me fix your hair."

Closing my eyes, I let Tavi comb my hair. She wrapped and tucked it and then held it in place with a pearl hair ornament she had found in a jewelry box. Then Tavi plucked flowers from the table and wove them into a braid. I wondered where she had learned this. Jewish women don't usually bother with hairstyles.

Their heads are always covered when they go out, and at home, they tie their hair back or braid it, nothing fancy.

Tavi stood back and gazed at me, arms folded across her chest.

"Esther," she whispered, "you look so grown up . . . and so pretty."

"Do you think so?"

I twirled around. Tavi nodded, staring. I liked pretending. It was fun, but as Tavi continued to stare, suddenly I felt uncomfortable. I wasn't sure why. Perhaps it was fear of her mother finding me in the gown.

"Enough of this! Now it's your turn!"

Tavi helped me out of the dress and lay it gently where she had found it, like laying down a sleeping baby, afraid of waking him.

"I don't think I want to try it on," Tavi said. "Let's find something else to do. Anyway, mother will return soon."

She was right. Minutes later Aunt Mehry entered the house carrying a basket filled with emerald green fabric, white lace and several spools of ribbon. Little Micah clutched the back of her skirt.

"Hello, girls," Aunt Mehry said as she set the basket on the table. "What have you been up to?"

She looked at me, startled. "My, what is this?" She turned me around by the shoulders. "One of my pearl hair ornaments? You girls have been in my workshop! I hope you didn't disturb anything."

With one hand on my shoulder and other on my chin, she turned my head to the side and studied Tavi's workmanship. "I'm impressed. Did you do this, Tavita?"

"Yes, mother."

"You did a very nice job, but next time, ask permission before going into my workshop. You know I don't like you in there. Esther, please put that back where you found it."

"Yes, ma'm," I said, avoiding her eyes. Then slowly I removed the flowers and pearl comb, and took them to the workroom. I ran my fingers through my hair, shaking my head gently to let it tumble over my shoulders.

"Esther," Aunt Mehry said as I returned to the kitchen tying my hair back. "As soon as Mordecai officially announces your betrothal, I will take you to the bazaar and buy you any jewelry you like so that when your new husband Asher removes your veil, you will dazzle him."

I felt my face grow hot, tears stinging my eyes. "I love you, Aunt Mehry. Thank you." I reached up and draped my arms around her, hugging her tightly.

Chapter 3

It had been three years since King Ahasuerus banished Queen Vashti from the throne. We had forgotten about that incident over time since it did not seem to have had any direct bearing on our daily lives, until one day that I would never forget as long as I live.

Cousin came home from his usual trip to the king's gate. Rather than sitting down and talking about the day, he paced through the house with his eyes down, and wrung his hands. "I will have no dinner tonight," was all he had to say for the longest time.

After going up onto the roof, perhaps to pray, he finally came back and said, "I've been troubled by an edict the king has posted throughout the empire. He intends to find a new queen to replace Vashti, and will make his selection from all the eligible virgins in Persia. I've been instructed to post this notice at each entrance of the marketplace." He handed a copy of it to me.

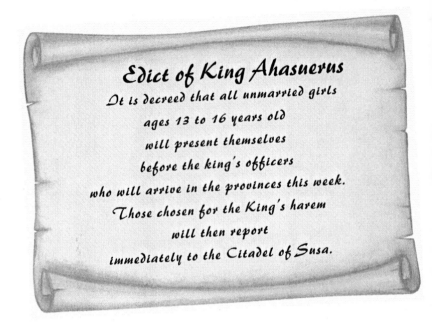

Edict of King Ahasuerus
It is decreed that all unmarried girls
ages 13 to 16 years old
will present themselves
before the king's officers
who will arrive in the provinces this week.
Those chosen for the King's harem
will then report
immediately to the Citadel of Susa.

At first, I was puzzled as to why Cousin was so upset, but he said, "Esther, you are a beautiful girl. Surely you won't escape their notice."

"What?" I cried. "But I'm a Jew, not a Persian!"

Cousin's voice was soft. "You are both a Jew and a Persian, Esther, but nationality makes no difference. In the king's harem there are women from many countries."

"But I'm nearly betrothed. What about that? And what about Asher? I want to marry him and have a normal family—not be in a harem. Tavi and I have planned to live next door to each other and watch our children play together."

He turned his back to me, lowering his head, slowly massaging his temples. "According to Persian law, Esther, you are eligible. Your betrothal has not been formalized. I shouldn't have waited. I should have moved more quickly with the arrangements. Jehovah in heaven, forgive me."

"Cousin, I could dress as a boy. I'll cut my hair right now." I hurried toward the toolbox where we kept our sharp implements, but he stepped in front of me and held my shoulders.

"You must not do that, Esther. You will be found out, and I will be beheaded for permitting your folly and protecting you. We will pray that Jehovah will blind the king's messengers when they pass by our home."

I grabbed his hands, pressing them tightly as if I could squeeze out of him the words I wanted to hear. "Please tell me what would happen if I were taken, yet the king disliked me. Could I come back home? Surely the king wouldn't miss me if he has so many women."

Mordecai closed his eyes and rubbed them with his fingertips. "If you were taken but not chosen as queen, I regret that you would remain in the harem as a concubine. This is the way of kings—not just here in Persia, but in Israel as well, all the way back to our first King Saul."

I was unwilling to accept his answer and pressed him again. "Cousin, could we run away and hide somewhere? I don't want to live with a lot of women in the palace, separated from those I love."

The aroma of bread baking floated in the window, and I looked out as if I could see where the smell was coming from. A neighbor—probably a happily married woman baking for the man she loves. In a quieter voice I asked, "Why couldn't the king choose one of the wives he already has to be the queen?"

Cousin took both of my hands in his. "Sometimes it is hard to understand life, Esther." Looking deeply into his eyes, I saw tears forming in the corners. He said, "I know it will be hard, but try to remember that even in a pagan land, Jehovah is still in control of everything that happens to us."

Suddenly I gasped, covering my mouth with my hand. "Oh Cousin! Suppose Tavita is taken and I am left behind. What will I do without her?" I buried my face in my hands and sobbed.

Dear Judah,

Perhaps I will go to sleep tonight and wake up in the morning to find this was a terrible dream. Queen Vashti! It is her fault! She should have obeyed the king's command and done as he requested. If Vashti had not been so proud or foolish, I would not have this misery. Three years ago, Vashti made a mistake that now others must pay for . . . I might have to pay for. Oh, Jehovah, deliver me from this fate. And Tavita—O Lord, blind the eyes of the king's servants that they might not see us.

I hardly slept that night and woke up the next morning with a pounding head. My whole body ached. I felt parched as if I had trudged through the desert for days without water. I sat on the side of my bed for several minutes hoping that the room would come into focus. Slowly I got up, slid into my sandals and shuffled to where Mordecai sat with his head in his hands. He looked up, and then rose to greet me. With dark circles under his eyes, he looked ten years older.

"My dear girl." He reached out to me, drawing me into a warm hug. "You were restless throughout the night."

I nodded my head against his firm chest as he stroked my head and said, "Here, have some tea. Would you like some cinnamon bread?"

"No bread, thank you, I don't feel like eating, but I will have some tea."

As he poured it from the steaming kettle into a cup, the scent of jasmine enveloped me like a soft blanket. When he set it before me on the table, I closed my eyes and inhaled deeply.

He spoke softly. "I went out early this morning. Talk of the king's edict seems to dominate everyone's conversation in the community."

"So it wasn't a bad dream." I wrapped both hands around my cup. "I had hoped to wake and discover that I had imagined all that trouble about the king and his harem."

Mordecai poured himself some tea and sat down across from me. "I also wish that were a dream. But not all families are distraught about the news." He shook his head and scratched behind his ear. "I hear that some girls are delighted at the idea of living in luxury in the harem."

"Not I! All I want is to celebrate every Passover and Sabbath with you and Tavita—she'll be right next door." I tried to sound hopeful, but the thought of being separated from her crept back into my mind and brought a fresh rush of tears spilling down my cheeks. Resting my head on my arms, I cried until I thought there could be no more tears inside of me. I was wrong.

Aunt Mehry appeared in our doorway, hands raised to heaven, and tears dropping as water from a fountain. "Why Jehovah? Why now?"

Mordecai rose to greet her and rested his hands on her arms as if to impart peace. "Nothing has happened yet, Mehry. Our girls are still with us," he said as he pulled out a chair for her. Mehry sat down. She looked older and more fragile than she had just one day ago. He continued. "The Persians have suffered a great defeat from their battles in Greece and perhaps the king's way of consoling himself is by finding a new queen. He and his navy have finally returned to Susa and perhaps it is time for him to dwell on new things."

Aunt Mehry shook her head. "If the king had chosen a new queen as soon as Vashti was sent away, our girls would have been too young to be considered. Or he could have waited another year and the girls could both have been married or betrothed." She rested her head on her hands. "Oh Jehovah, spare us and our children!"

Dear Judah,

The selections have begun. When the king's officers look over the girls, they take whomever they please. At the bazaar, I heard two Persian women gloating to their friends that their daughters were chosen. They think it is a great honor. Dinah said that perhaps the parents were glad to get rid of them so they would not have to pay a dowry to marry them off.

But not me, Lord Jehovah! If I were chosen, I would have to leave those I love and never get to come back. My life would be over. I would never get to make a nice home for Asher. And the king worships idols and has different customs. No one at the palace is Jewish; no one would care about Passovers and my special holidays. They would not care about my dreams to go to Jerusalem one day.

"The Lord loves the gates of Zion
more than all the dwellings of Jacob.
Glorious things are spoken of you,
O city of God!"

Oh, I pray that the king's messenger will think I'm too plain to be considered for the harem, in spite of what Cousin says. I will stay up all night and pray that Jehovah will deliver me from this awful fate.

I eventually fell asleep that night after periods of prayer and tears, tears and prayer and more tears. In the morning, the king's officers went throughout my neighborhood demanding that parents bring out all eligible girls. I stood in the doorway of our house next to Mordecai and kept my eyes to the ground. My hands were damp, clenched tightly in front of me.

The officer approached me, lifted up my chin with his hand, and looked closely at my face, then over my body. He made me remove my veil and felt my hair. I wanted to run and hide from him, but even if I thought I could get away, my legs had no strength to run. I felt humiliated at the way he looked at me and stroked my hair.

Then the man said to Mordecai, "You will bring the girl to the Citadel tomorrow at sunrise. She will go into the harem of the great and glorious King Ahasuerus." He turned suddenly and moved on to the next house.

I stood as a statue, letting his words run through my mind until the shock of what had happened startled me like being awakened in the middle of the night. With his arm around my shoulders, Mordecai led me into our home. Pounding my fists into Mordecai's chest, I sobbed until I fell exhausted onto my bed. I slept until dusk and awakened, thinking morning had come. I sat on the side of my bed and could hear my cousin mumbling in the other room. I knew he was in prayer but charged in anyway.

"Why did this happen and why do you pray now? Jehovah did not hear our prayers. He has forgotten me. He should have protected me."

Cousin held me close, but I would not be comforted. "I am UGLY. Why don't they leave me alone to live out my life as an ordinary woman?"

"Esther, Esther. I don't know." He spoke just above a whisper. "I wish I had an answer for you. I know only that the king's orders must be obeyed under penalty of death. You must go, my beloved child. I don't know how I can bear to be without you. You have been my life these last years. I'm sorry for us both."

Suddenly, with a mixture of terror and hope, I ran outside into the darkening street to Tavi's house to see if she had been selected also. She stood in her doorway, her arms hanging straight by her side and shook her head. "You?" she asked me with a knowing look.

I nodded. Tavi grabbed and held me while we both sobbed inconsolably. Aunt Mehry gathered us both in her embrace and joined in our wailing.

"My daughter, Esther. Our love will be with you every day. When we look at the night sky, we will search out the brightest and most beautiful star, and think of you. But you must also consider your Mordecai, whose heart is surely broken even as ours."

Tavi and her mother walked me home, and we stood crying at my threshold. I thought we might never see each other again after tomorrow.

Cousin gently pulled us apart. "Mehry, please get your husband and son, and join us for this last meal together. Tavi, you stay and help Esther."

We could have watered a garden with all the tears we shed that day.

Later that evening, Mordecai spoke in a hushed voice. "Perhaps it won't be so bad. You are a lovely young woman and the king would be foolish not to realize that no one is more beautiful inside and outside than you are." He faced me and said in a firm voice, "Regardless of the outcome, Esther, do not tell anyone that you are Jewish. There are people who hate us because our religious practices are so different from others in Persia. Some mistrust anyone who doesn't worship the same gods as they do. It is as the scripture tells us in a psalm, 'We have become a reproach to our neighbors, a scorn and derision to those who are around us.'"

"Cousin, do you think it's possible for me to keep my Jewishness concealed?"

"You need to at least try, Esther."

"They will make me offer sacrifices to Anahita the earth goddess. How can I worship Jehovah in secret while those around me worship Ahura-Mazda? It's bad enough that his image is everywhere, looking like a winged sun. Even their diet is different from ours. What will I do, Cousin Mordecai?"

He stroked my head as I buried my face in his shoulder and cried, but quietly. "You can attend the worship and do what is necessary," he said, "but keep your mind and heart on Jehovah. He will sanctify the foods you eat and the servants may allow you to eat whatever you like—if you treat them well."

I sat staring off into the distance as he continued. "Esther, I'm sure that we'll see each other again," he said. "The Citadel's guards are familiar with me and will allow me access to the courtyard. Surely there's a way I can daily check on your welfare."

I found some comfort in Mordecai's promise that he would come every day to see how I was doing, even if we were not permitted to talk. Who would look after my dear cousin? I couldn't bear thinking about missing my morning walks to the bazaar with Tavi. A million questions plagued my mind.

Word spread quickly in our community, and shortly, Asher came to our home looking sullen. "Mordecai, may I have permission to speak to Esther?"

"Yes, of course. Please come in."

Asher took my arm and led me out to the courtyard behind our home. Clouds were dissipating, revealing the starry sky.

"I had to come as soon as I heard," he said in a raspy voice. He shook his head slowly and raised both hands as if he were pleading with heaven.

"I've loved you, Esther, since the first time I saw you and prayed that someday we could marry. When we were about to be betrothed, I celebrated with my friends and my joy increased all the more when you told me of your desire to go to Judah one day, because that has also been my wish for as long as I can remember."

With my eyes to the floor, I wrapped my arms around myself and rocked back and forth on my heels.

Asher continued. "Jehovah has given you great beauty, so it is no surprise that you will go to the king. I will be praying that it goes well for you in his household, and that you will have favor with all those who will attend you. My thoughts will always be with you."

My eyes stung with tears and my throat tightened as though I were being strangled. I lifted my head to look at him.

"Thank you, Asher," I finally managed. "I hope that you will fulfill your dream of going to Jerusalem one day. Our generation must continue to rebuild Jerusalem and become a great nation again."

He nodded. "I will . . ." A single tear dropped onto his cheek. He brushed it away with his thumb and put his hands on my shoulders. Asher looked into my eyes for a moment, then leaned toward me and kissed my forehead.

"Goodbye, Esther. Jehovah be with you." He turned and walked away, nodding to Mordecai who stood watching by the door.

Dear Judah,

Since I must not let anyone know I am a Jewess, I must think of a new name for my chronicles. Perhaps I will address them as "Dooste man," "my friend," for this scroll will be as a companion and the only possession I will take with me to the Citadel of Susa and the harem of the king.

Tonight, before I went to bed for the last time in Mordecai's home, he told me that our dreams are not always what Jehovah has planned for our lives. Since I have been chosen, we must believe that this is Jehovah's will for me, my destiny. What lies ahead? I cannot imagine that I will ever be happy again.

Chapter 4

WALKING TO THE CITADEL THE NEXT MORNING, I FELT AS THOUGH I WAS walking toward my death. I could have ridden in the king's carriage, but I wanted to feel under my feet the dirt of familiar roads and hold onto each memory, if only for a few minutes more.

With each step, I saw the faces of those I love fade into a gray, watery, cloud. Tavi clung to her mother, wailing when I passed. She called after me, "I'll never forget you, Esther. Never!"

I held tightly to my cousin's arm as we slowly made our way down one street, then another. The scent of baking Challah drifted from homes where women prepared for tomorrow's Sabbath meal. Each member of the household would repeat the words, "Blessed art thou, O Lord Jehovah, King of the Universe, who brings forth bread from the earth." King of the Universe—that includes Persia, I reminded myself.

We walked on as houses and shops disappeared behind us. Passing the silversmith's shop where Asher worked, I looked for him in the doorway, but he was not there. Inside, I saw the shadow of a man with bowed head seated at a table, and then that image also blended into a dense fog.

We finally drew near to the main entrance of the Citadel. The arched doorway was as high as three men, and the parapets appeared to almost touch the clouds. The towering walls were smooth except for small windows where we saw guards at their posts. It looked more like a prison than my new home.

Two of the sentries, who had been watching us approach, stepped toward us abruptly, one hand gripping the handle of a sword, the other hand extended toward Cousin.

"Far enough," one said looking severely at Mordecai. "Move on now!"

Another sentry nodded toward me.

"This way."

I removed my hand from Mordecai's arm. He patted my hand then bowed and kissed it. He backed away, not taking his eyes from mine.

"This way!" called the sentry.

I nodded and stepped toward him. I had to bite down on my tongue to keep my composure and then followed a few steps behind the soldier. Glancing over my shoulder as I passed through the entrance of the Citadel, I saw Mordecai backing away, watching me, hand raised in a limp wave.

I thought of the day, several years earlier, when I had watched my parents carried away on biers, side-by-side, in their funeral procession. Thousands of people died during that plague, and I used to wish I had died with them. I lost my beloved parents and now had to say goodbye to my cousin who had become my father.

Continuing to follow the sentry through a courtyard and up a long flight of stairs, I wondered how I could live when all those I had known and loved had been stripped away from me . . . all except Jehovah. His love must replace everything I had lost.

I entered a large room full of women. Some were clearly servants; others were young women looking uneasy, and a few were smiling and boisterous. It was noisy, but I hardly understood more than a word here and there—I was not listening to the babbling voices. It was as though I were deaf.

As darkness fell over the city, intermittent loud booms reverberated through the harem, startling me. "What is that?" I asked a servant.

"Just the gates. The gates are sealed for the night."

The next day was the Sabbath. I wouldn't be there to see Aunt Mehry light the first candle. "This candle represents creation," she would say. "Blessed art Thou, O Lord Jehovah, King of the Universe, who brings forth light out of darkness." I imagined I could hear Mordecai chanting his prayers as I lay awake sobbing in the strange bed until the sun rose. I had hoped that my red, puffy eyes and lack of sleep would make the attendants think I was ugly and send me back home in the morning, but no one seemed to notice.

Knowing that Mordecai would try to visit me was a comfort, but those first days in the harem, I could not eat anything even though it looked wonderful. Flat bread with Cousin Mordecai would have made me happier.

Chapter 5

MOST OF THE GIRLS SEEMED HAPPY TO BE AT THE PALACE. THEY WERE all so pretty, although no one was familiar to me. I looked in vain for an acquaintance, but the faces were all of strangers. Since the empire extended all the way west to Greece and Egypt, and east to India, there were girls of many nationalities and cultures, and we would all be trained in the ways of the king's court.

After several days, my appetite gradually returned and I began to enjoy the juicy citrus fruits, some varieties that I had never seen before, and lamb flavored with tamarind from India.

The girls talked continually as they tried to decide who was the prettiest and who would be chosen as queen.

"Niyaf will be chosen since she is tall and graceful, as well as beautiful," one said. Several others agreed with her.

Alya stood with one hand behind her head and the other hand on a hip, face tilting upward. "Have you not noticed me? My wavy hair is as soft as the finest silk and as black as the darkest onyx. I shall be the king's favorite."

Her features and figure were, indeed, beautiful, but her mouth wore a scowl that detracted from her appearance. It reminded me of a proverb about a jewel in a pig's snout.

When I was a child, Cousin told me to be less interested regarding outward beauty and more concerned with showing kindness to others. Some of the girls in the harem had apparently not learned this, as they were not very kind at all. They pushed and shoved to have first choice of clothes and jewelry, although every item was more beautiful than anything I had ever seen. Alya scratched another girl's arm when she grabbed for a sapphire necklace.

Dooste man,

For some reason that I don't understand, Hegai, the king's servant in charge of the harem, has set aside special things just for me and has assigned seven maids to wait on me when the other girls have only two or three. Holding an emerald in my hand for the first time in my life, I thought of the smooth, colored stones Tavi and I used to throw in the river to commemorate Tashlich. Sometimes these stones were so pretty that we wanted to keep them in our pockets. Then Cousin would remind us that sometimes our sins also seemed nice, but the Lord wanted us to get rid of them. We understood then why this tradition was important to our faith.

Rashad, one of my maids, arranges my hair in different styles and uses ornate combs, strings of pearls, and sometimes flowers to make me look beautiful. Her gentleness reminds me of long ago when I sat cross-legged on the floor in front of my mother as she brushed my hair, making my scalp tingle and my eyes close involuntarily. My body slowly, very slowly, would slump down at her feet. Later, I would find myself on my bed, not sure how I got there. Momma must have picked me up and carried me there after I had fallen asleep.

I was so young then, practically a baby. But since momma's death, I have taken care of my hair myself, except for the time Tavi and I dressed each other's hair, pretending to be the queen.

After several weeks in the harem, I became accustomed to being pampered. One of my maids, Furat, prepared oils to make my skin soft and applied fragrant perfumes to make me smell like a garden in bloom.

"Mistress," she said one day. "There is a sorrow in your heart that dulls your eyes, the way a cloudy day obscures the brilliance of flowers in a garden. But I promise if you will eat the pomegranates and fresh vegetables I bring you every day, it will brighten your complexion and make your eyes sparkle. You will forget the sorrow of the past."

"You are kind, Furat, and your words are a comfort to me, but no food can lighten my heart."

She was not the only one who noticed my melancholy spirit. Hegai, the head chamberlain, gave me the best apartment in the virgins' section of the harem. As servants brought my clothes, perfumes and toiletries into my new quarters, Hegai surprised me by asking, "Esther, would you like to be queen?"

"That is a strange question, Hegai. I cannot imagine myself being chosen above all the others. Everyone here is so beautiful and I have nothing that makes me special."

"Esther, you can rise like a star above all the other women. Only one thing holds you back—your regret for what you left behind. You're here now," he said, pointing to the floor, "and you'll never return to your family and friends, so you must accept that fact and look ahead to the future. Life can be good for you here, and I will look after you by making sure you have the best of everything. I'll make a queen out of you."

I listened to each word and considered them as I turned away from him, walking out to the terrace. Below there were gardens, a courtyard with a fountain, and beyond that, the gated wall. "Left behind . . . never return . . . the future." His words echoed in my head, and I realized that the most significant word he used was "accept." I had to face the fact that my former life had ended, and if I wanted to make the most of my future, I had to do all that I could to be the best that I could be.

Hegai stood beside me on the terrace and looked out toward the open gate, but at dusk, it would be closed and locked for the night. He continued, "A half-hearted attempt, applying make-up and wearing beautiful clothes will never hide the sadness inside of you." He put his hand on my arm. "In your heart you must want to move on. The rest of your life depends on the choice you make today. Would you rather be one of a hundred concubines or the queen of Persia?"

My answer was becoming clearer as I considered the difference between a concubine, a slave woman who could have legitimate sexual relations with her master but still did not have the rights of a free wife; whereas, some wives may have significant influence on their husbands, but being one of many wives would certainly diminish their privileges. But to be queen of Persia? I had never really considered that possibility.

"Hegai, do you think it's conceivable that I could be the one?"

He paused a moment before speaking, but I could see in his eyes that he knew it could happen. He turned to face me and then nodded. "Yes, it could happen. Are you ready to work toward that end?" he said.

I could not immediately give him the answer he wanted. I took a deep, slow breath knowing that I had to abandon all hope of returning to the life I had previously in order to look ahead with a new vision. "Ask me again tomorrow."

Hegai bowed—for the first time—then went to the door. "Until tomorrow, My lady."

As I lay in bed that night, I went over every word that Hegai had spoken to me. Before that day I had not seriously believed that I had a chance to be chosen as queen, but if Hegai believed it was possible, then I would work hard at doing my best to learn all I could from him.

The next morning, I smiled at Hegai as to a mentor rather than a foe.

"I am ready."

He smiled. "Let us begin then."

Chapter 6

HEGAI TAUGHT ME THE PROPER WAY TO WALK AND TO MOVE AS IF I were walking through a garden carpeted with rose petals. "Pretend there is a string attached to the top of your head to lift you up," he said. "Glide, do not tromp. I can pull you up by your hair if you need help remembering."

"No, thank you," I said, stretching myself as far as I could.

Later in the day, I strolled through a garden accompanied by Furat, Rashad and Safiya, recalling the time Tavita and I played "dress up" with a wedding gown. What would it be like to marry a king, I wondered. How elaborate would that wedding be? The weddings I had experienced were the week-long celebrations of Jewish couples that were wonderful. We danced, sang, and ate until we collapsed. Would a Persian king dance and sing? I had no idea. One thing I was sure of was that there would be extravagant gifts, more than I could ever imagine.

A courier handed a note to Safiya with instructions to give it to me. He stood, awaiting a reply. She handed it to me. "My lady."

I knew what it must be—I recognized Mordecai's handwriting and quickly unrolled the note. My heart nearly stopped beating and I paused to catch my breath. The note said,

"Can you meet me along the wall by the western gate?"

"Safiya, please tell the messenger, the answer is 'yes.'"

She turned and walked to him with my answer. Even as she did this, I was unsure about how I would explain my meeting with Mordecai to the maids. As we continued to the other side of the garden toward the wall, I said, "Furat and Rashad, please return to my apartment and prepare the bath. I'm very warm and would like to freshen up before the evening meal."

They responded in unison, "Yes, my lady," then turned and left.

Safiya walked a few steps behind me until I sat on a bench near the western gate. I felt that I could trust her since I could not have been alone with Mordecai.

My entire body quivered with anticipation and my breaths struggled to keep up with the beating of my heart. My eyes searched the path until I saw him approaching. Mordecai's steps were slow but purposeful. Our eyes locked, and I rose as I felt all the warmth of my affection spurring me toward him.

A voice spoke in my head, Stop! Suddenly confused about how I could greet this most important man in my life and yet hide all that emotion and love, I stood still, bowing my head with my eyes closed.

Safiya's voice broke into my thoughts. "My lady, may I get something for you? Perhaps you should sit down."

I put my hand on her arm. "No, I am all right. If you would please step aside for a few moments, I must speak with my old friend."

She looked at Mordecai, then nodded and strolled a short distance away.

"Cousin, it's wonderful to see you. I've missed you so." I grasped his arm.

He patted my hand and smiled. "How does it go with you, my dear Esther? Are you treated well? Have you been eating? Sleeping? Tell me. But I can stay here only a few minutes."

I laughed to hear him rattle off the questions without giving me an opportunity to respond. "Not so bad," I lied. "And yes, no and no."

Mordecai smiled and shook his head. "I'm sorry, Esther. I suppose I got carried away by seeing you."

I told him about all the exceptional treatment I had been receiving from Hegai.

In a low voice, he said, "It is because you have Jehovah's favor, Esther. Pay close attention to all that Hegai tells you to do, because he knows what the king likes and will instruct you well."

Dooste man,

For the first time since coming to the Citadel, I slept soundly, and today, feeling adventurous, I spent some time exploring the harem and Citadel. On the high windows there are purple linen draperies pulled back with cords onto silver rings. I have never before seen anything like the tapestries that hang on the walls. Many of them are threaded with gold and embroidered with scenes of flower gardens and birds. I recall watching women weave them at the bazaar when I went there with dear Tavita. Oh, how I miss her.

Surrounding the garden in the courtyard is a marble sidewalk, and in the center is a fountain with lions carved from limestone standing at each end as if they were guarding the precious water. Mosaic-tiled floors with multi-colored, elaborate designs are almost too beautiful to walk on.

As lovely as this is, it cannot be as wonderful as the temple in Jerusalem was when King Solomon built it and the cloud of Jehovah's presence filled the entire place. It was so powerful that the people fell on their faces as they worshipped, and King Solomon proclaimed:

"The Lord said He would dwell in the dark cloud. I have surely built You an exalted house and a place for You to dwell in forever."

"Forever . . ." Though the Babylonians destroyed it, Jehovah's presence has continued through the generations to be with us somehow. As a nation we have rebelled against Him, but He never forgets us, and eventually we rise again from oppression. I do not understand why He is so merciful toward us, but I am grateful to be His child.

The king's chamberlains had charge over the women in the harem and saw to it that we lacked nothing. There were three sections within the harem. For the first year of preparation, I was with the virgins, and we were not permitted in the area set apart for the concubines, those women who served the king but were not his wives.

In another section, the king's wives had apartments that were large and luxurious, surpassed only by the queen's quarters that were unequaled in comfort and beauty. King Ahasuerus would eventually choose one of the virgins to be the new queen. All the other women would spend the rest of their lives without a husband but be well taken care of. Perhaps they would be content, but I always wondered why he did not just pick a queen from among his wives. It seemed that would have been easier; then the rest of us could have stayed with our families. However, that was not the way of King Ahasuerus.

Dooste man,

Safiya and I spend a lot of time together. She is becoming my favorite maid because she is not only helpful to me but seems trustworthy and genuinely cares for me. Today we walked together through a lovely orchard in the courtyard at the center of the house. Olive, palm, and cypress trees grow there, in addition to pomegranates and flowers I could not identify. Safiya is intelligent and knows them all by name, teaching me as we walk along. Anemone Caronaria is the flower I like best with its crimson petals and deep green leaves. The Adonis Palestina looks so fragile with its wispy fern-like leaves and small red petals. In contrast, there is the sturdy, yellow-gold Chrysanthemum. The wonders of creation frequently remind me of the One who gave us all this beauty.

In spite of the exquisite surroundings, I missed Cousin Mordecai and dear Tavi. I also missed Dinah, Mehira and the other women I used to see each morning. I even wished I could listen to them arguing. In the past, I used to think it would be nice to be pampered, but now I longed for the old ways with my own people. I continued to keep my Jewish heritage secret, even from Safiya.

One morning when she and I were alone, I asked, "Safiya, do you ever miss your family and childhood friends the way I do?"

"Oh, yes, my lady," she said almost in a whisper. She looked off into the distance as though searching for that far-off city.

"How is it that you came here to serve in the harem of Ahasuerus?"

Looking down at her slim, graceful hands, she said, "My family had at one time been prosperous—not greatly, but comfortably. Then after a blight wiped out our crops, we struggled even to have enough food." Her hand went self-consciously to her stomach. "My brothers were younger than I and were not yet able to contribute, so I helped by repairing torn clothes for neighbors and doing errands at the market, but it was not enough."

I could almost see the hunger in her eyes as she related the story.

"Since I was of age to be betrothed, and my father had no money for a dowry, he brought me to the Citadel to be a servant. Since that day two years ago, I have not seen friend or family and I miss them, of course, but this is the life that has been allotted to me.

"You serve well, Safiya—perhaps with more dedication than anyone else," I said. "I am grateful to have you here even though it has not been of your choosing."

"Thank you, my lady."

Hegai joined us and then dismissed Safiya since it was time for his daily instruction. In addition to etiquette training, he wanted me to learn about Persia's history and conquests, so he taught me about the king's ancestors, King Cyrus the Great and King Darius."

"These were both great warriors who expanded the empire all the way past the River Euphrates to the Nile River in Egypt, then toward the east to India."

I was not interested too much in all the details about the wars, but I learned as much as I could. Hegai told me how King Cyrus had acknowledged the Lord God of Heaven and permitted the Jewish prophet Ezra to take any family who wanted to return to Judah and rebuild the temple in Jerusalem. When Hegai said this,

I felt my face flush and my heart burn inside of me. I wanted to say to him, "Yes, this is my God, Jehovah, whom I know and worship!" Nevertheless, in spite of the pounding of my heart, I kept silent.

Hegai looked at me strangely, squinting. "Esther, do you feel feverish?" He handed me a glass of water.

Taking the glass and sipping, I said, "No, please go on. I want to hear more."

He continued the story about King Cyrus, the story I already knew so well; but I listened as if it were the first time I had ever heard it.

Another day I learned something that would have a profound effect on my life, although at the time I had no way of knowing that. It was regarding how the laws of the land were made and enforced.

"Once written," Hegai informed me, "a law of the Medes and Persians, stamped with the king's signet ring, cannot be revoked under any circumstances."

"Isn't there some way of allowing exceptions in case conditions or rulers change?"

"No," said Hegai. "There are no exceptions. The laws are 'written in stone.'"

I considered that for a long moment, realizing how quickly lives—individually like my own, and that of a nation—could change. It seemed impractical to have irrevocable laws, but perhaps I did not understand all the implications that might arise. After all, I was just beginning to learn about the things of the world.

After my time with Hegai, I went with Rashad, Furat and Safiya to a far corner of the Citadel and watched for a long time while a stone carver chiseled a frieze onto a wall. Many future generations will see the work of this artisan.

I said to my maids, "What a privilege that man has—to be a part of history, telling a story for others to 'read' for, perhaps, thousands of years. I wonder if anything in my life will be remembered, or will I pass through my time on earth making little difference to anyone?"

I looked over at the wall as I remembered my friend Tavita who might forget me after a few years. I hoped not, but it was possible that only my cousin would remember me. Suddenly, I felt ashamed because Rashad, Furat and Safiya would be servants all their lives until they were too old and then just wait to die—and who would remember a servant?

"I'm sorry," I said to them. "Forgive me for thinking only of myself."

They nodded, but I noticed the sadness in Safiya's eyes—a far away longing."

None of the carvings throughout the city included images of women. They were always of men, either fighting in battles or showing homage to a king or various gods with worshippers presenting offerings of goats, rams and other animals. Since I was not permitted to speak to the man, I said, "Safiya, ask the stone carver why there are no women."

She asked him and he replied, "Women are not important—beautiful, yes, but important, no." He winked at her and she blushed.

When we returned to the harem, we were covered with dust. Hegai looked aghast when he saw us and said to waste no time in cleaning up. We laughed as we hurried off to the baths. I enjoyed getting dirty for a change.

I stared at my reflection with my hair looking ashen gray.

"Rashad, I know now how I will look when I grow old."

She said smiling, "With all the beauty treatments you receive, my lady, you will never look old."

Dooste man,

I have now been here almost a year and Hegai continues to give me special privileges. I have enjoyed the nicest apartment of all the virgins, though some of the young women resent me for it, especially Alya. She turns her head when I approach and stops talking when I try to enter into conversations. I don't like being shunned, but I still have my maids who always surround me. Abeer, Samra, Safiya, and the others tend to my every need. It is nice to be pampered, but sometimes I would like to be alone and not have such a fuss made over the way I look.

I continued in my study of Persian history. Hegai said, "King Darius, Ahasuerus' father, believed he was appointed by the god Ahura-Mazda to build a canal between the Red Sea and the Nile River. He did this to make traveling easier between east and west, thereby providing an excellent method of bringing Egypt's gold to Persia."

Safiya worships this god, Ahura-Mazda, but in spite of that, I have taught her one of King David's verses, not mentioning that King David was a Jew, only that he lived long ago in another country.

"To the upright there arises light in the darkness,
He is gracious, and full of compassion, and righteous."

"Mistress, to whom does the verse refer?" Safiya asked.

I replied, "To the God of Heaven." I wanted to tell her about Jehovah, but I promised Cousin I would not reveal my Jewish ancestry, so I had to be faithful to my word. It was hard to keep a secret from my friend, like holding back the water from flowing to the sea. As I meditated on King David's words, I found my heart feeling lighter. Jehovah brought light into my darkness by giving me a new friend and Hegai who looked after me in much the way Cousin Mordecai had.

When I stopped feeling sorry for myself, I began to notice things in the other people who surrounded me, particularly Safiya. She was sweet and gentle as a mother would be although not much older than I, and she moved with grace. However, there was no sparkle in her eyes, perhaps because of her state in life as a maid. I determined to discover what it was, so one day when we were alone I asked her, "Safiya, what causes the sorrow that I sometimes see in your face? Is it longing for your family?"

She drew back in fear. "Sorrow? Oh no, mistress. You are mistaken."

Perhaps another day she would allow me to share her secret. It was difficult for me to think of her just as a servant—someone to cater to every whim of mine. I wanted her as a friend, although I didn't know if that was possible.

One day as Rashad, Safiya and I strolled through a garden near the entrance to the Citadel, I noticed Cousin speaking to some other men and a guard. Mordecai continued to come daily to the gate of the courtyard to see that I was well. He would pace back and forth there until I could break away from everyone and meet him. He wore a practiced smile, but I could see the pain in his eyes, even from a distance.

I refrained from running to him, for fear of attracting attention, but I grabbed his arm, almost squeezing the life from him, as we walked close to the wall.

"Are they treating you well, my dear?" he asked.

"They treat me too well. The maids never leave me alone except when they think I am asleep. Oh Cousin, how I long to sit in our home and listen to you pray in the early morning or to stand alone on our rooftop and watch the stars."

He nodded as I told him how Hegai continued to pamper and instruct me. He seemed pleased. "Esther, I want you to wear the smile that I love so dearly. Stand erect," he lifted my chin, "and know that Jehovah is with you, as well as my love and constant prayers. Who knows where all this may lead you?"

We walked in silence for a few minutes. Cousin looked at the ground and stroked his beard continuously until we came to a bench.

"Let's sit down, Esther." We both sat down, but he was on the edge of the seat and had his hands folded between his knees.

"What's troubling you, Cousin? "

"I have news from our neighbor Moshe. He has announced the betrothal between his daughter Tavita and Asher the silversmith."

I stared at him as though he had spoken a foreign language I did not understand. It took a few moments until the reality of his words sunk into my mind.

"How could they betray me?"

Cousin tried to take my hand, but I stood up with my back to him and folded my arms across my chest. I tasted salt from the hot tears that slid down my face and brushed them away with the back of my hand.

Mordecai waited quietly for a while, and then spoke barely above a whisper.

"Esther, do you remember the last time you spoke to Asher—almost a year ago—when you gave him your blessing and encouraged him to pursue his dream?"

I nodded, but did not turn to face him. "But I didn't think that he would ask my best friend—"

"Tavita is, indeed, your friend, and for that reason don't you want her to marry a good man?"

"Yes, but it hurts, Cousin. My life-long dreams have been crushed."

"I know, but you're thinking only of yourself, not their happiness," he said.

Dooste man,

I know I am foolish to feel jealous for what Tavita now has. I have been in the harem nearly a year, and I know I cannot expect them to spend their lives mourning my loss.

I love Tavita more than anyone except Mordecai and I do want her to be happy, but what troubles me is realizing my dream has been lost forever. I will never be a Jewish wife and live the life I had expected. They will probably move to Jerusalem to fulfill Asher's plan. My mind accepts this as inevitable, but my heart does not.

With Furat's help, I completed my six months of treatments with oil of myrrh, and an additional six months with perfumes and special make-up applied by Rashad. Hegai taught me how to conduct myself in the king's presence and how to please him. Since my knowledge of men was very limited, Hegai patiently opened these new doors of life to me, although I often found it embarrassing.

Hegai said, "Esther, you must get over your shyness because it will hinder you from enjoying the king. Be yourself, and you'll surely be the king's favorite." He winked at me.

I wanted to believe him, but I was afraid to because there were so many beautiful girls for the king to choose from. I told Hegai about the day when Tavita and I saw Queen Vashti, and a neighbor told me that I was "too clumsy to be a fine lady."

"We'll prove her wrong, Esther," he said. "That woman would probably not recognize you today."

Four years had passed since that day with Tavita, and many things were different about me. It hardly seemed possible that my life could have changed so drastically. Back then, all I cared about was keeping house for my dear cousin and baking Sabbath bread, but in the harem, I did nothing for others except allow them to wait on me. It didn't seem right. Surely, Jehovah created me for more than that.

Dooste man,

Hegai had a special surprise for me today—he took me to visit Anusheh, one of the king's wives. She was lovely and moved gracefully. Her shiny, sable hair was adorned with pearls interwoven in braids and her pink skin looked almost transparent. Hegai asked her to speak to me about ways to please King Ahasuerus, since Anusheh is one of his favorites. She spoke kindly and patiently, without showing any signs of jealousy toward me. What a strange world this is.

I had not thought about it before, but Anusheh said that though Ahasuerus is king, he is first a man, and that I must make him believe there is no one else on earth I would rather be with. That will take a lot of concentration.

My time with Anusheh puzzled me even more as to why the king did not elevate her to the position as queen. I doubt that he will ever find a woman who loves him more or is more devoted to him. She has born him three children—two of them sons—and she is still young enough to give him more. Royalty is so different from a common life. I would prefer commonness to wealth within a harem, but the choice is not mine to make.

Dooste man,

Niyaf went to the king tonight. Her complexion was radiant and her gown was dark blue like the night sky. I must admit that she is the loveliest so far of all the girls taken to see the king. He is sure to be pleased with her.

The virgins' apartments are much quieter than they used to be, since most of the girls have moved to another part of the harem. Once they spent a night with the king, they were not permitted to return. I would have liked to ask the others what they thought of the king and find out how he treated them, but that is not possible. At least I still have my maids and a few of the women to keep me company . . . for now.

Chapter 7

THE NIGHT FINALLY CAME FOR MY TURN TO VISIT THE KING. IT WAS IN Jehovah's hands whether I would be cast aside to live as one of many wives, a concubine in the royal harem, or be selected as the most favored of the king and be his queen. However it turns out, I will never be the same.

"Be with me, Lord Jehovah," I whispered, as Safiya adorned my hair with an enameled ornament that looked like a peacock with colorful plumes and accented in gold.

"Now you are ready," Safiya said.

As the sun began to set, Hegai came to escort me to the king.

Leaving the virgins' quarters for the last time, my heart pounded as I passed by admiring chamberlains, maids and the other girls who stood with hands clasped at their chests, eyes sparkling with delight. They said, "Esther, you are so beautiful."

"Thank you, and thank you for serving me so faithfully this last year."

I walked through long corridors covered with sculptures in multi-colored, glazed stone. The images of warriors and ambassadors giving homage seemed to come alive as I passed. There were carvings of birds on gold lanterns. As light flickered through the lanterns, the birds appeared to take flight—right into the heavens, and the scent of sweet incense intoxicated me.

As I continued walking, I recited to myself a passage from The Songs of King Solomon.

"There are sixty queens
And eighty concubines.
And virgins without number.
My dove, my perfect one,
Is the only one,
The only one of her mother.
The favorite of the one who bore her.
The daughters saw her
And called her blessed,
The queens and the concubines,
And they praised her."

I was sure the sound of my pounding heart echoed in the marble hall. It seemed inconceivable that I, the Jewish maid Esther, was on my way to spend an evening with the great King Ahasuerus, ruler of the Persian Empire. I looked down at the bouquet of Damask roses in my hand and inhaled the sweet fragrance. With my other hand I smoothed the shimmering silver sash that encircled the waist of my amethyst silk gown, its skirt floating like a cloud as I stepped nearer to the waiting king.

Hegai and I stood at the entrance of the king's quarters. He turned to me and without speaking, smiled and bowed. Then we faced the king, knelt and bowed as the king's servant announced me.

"Your Majesty, I present Esther, daughter of Mordecai of the great city of Susa."

Hegai took several steps backward. He turned only when he reached the door. I heard his steps fading slowly as another phase of my life melted into the past.

King Ahasuerus sat on a high-backed chair of crimson velvet with his feet resting on a stool. At first, he seemed to pay little attention to me. He looked distant with his eyes half closed and his head tilted in his hand. Perhaps he was lost in his thoughts or the music of the lute. I thought to myself that maybe he was getting tired of one girl after the other and was losing interest. Would it be over before it started?

Then suddenly, the king sat up straight and smiled slightly as I approached him, his gaze sweeping over me from head to toe. I stopped when I came within reach of his scepter. Could he hear the pounding of my heart? He rose from his throne and extended his hand to me, lifting me up. I let out a slow, deep sigh as I stood to my feet.

"Your name is . . . Esther?" he asked.

"Yes, Your Majesty," I said. I liked the way he pronounced my name, as if he were rolling the sound of each letter around on his tongue and lips.

"What does Esther mean?"

"Your Majesty, it means 'Star.'"

"Star," he said. "Fitting. You have stars in your eyes, and your jewels look like stars circling your neck and wrists. You are beautiful."

Then bowing slightly, he kissed my hand and fingertips. One year. One year I prepared for this moment. I could hardly breathe.

He smiled and I felt a shiver run down my spine as he removed the veil from my face and head. Lifting my eyes, I dared to look directly at him. While outlining my face with soft fingers, his dark eyes reflected the flickering candlelight and reminded me of the shooting stars I had watched from my rooftop so long ago. His shining black hair curled around his face, blending into his beard.

"Your skin is softer than the petals of the roses you carry, Esther," he said as he kissed my cheek.

He signaled to his attendant who took the bouquet from me. The servant backed away several steps, bowed, and left the room, closing the door behind him. I could hear musicians playing softly in an adjoining room partitioned off by a wispy curtain.

King Ahasuerus loosened my braids that had been wrapped on my head like a crown, and my hair tumbled to my waist. He combed his fingers through my hair while I took slow breaths, trying to quiet the pounding of my heart. Anusheh's words floated into my consciousness, "as if we were the only two people on earth." Could so gentle a man also be a fierce warrior and harsh ruler? It did not seem possible. My thoughts melted away as the candles burned into pools, their last flickers of light abandoning their struggle to stay alive. My love and I sipped wine, and nibbled cheese and mandrakes, eventually falling asleep as first light crept over the windowsill.

When I awoke, the sun was blazing through the window. Ahasuerus rested on his side gazing at me making no attempt to hide his pleasure. I smiled up at him, holding his glance, feeling contented and happy.

Servants brought in a sumptuous breakfast on silver trays and poured Chaai from a silver carafe adorned with embossed bouquets. Our eyes met often as we lifted glinting cups to our lips. When we finished, the king kissed me on both cheeks and my right hand. He moved around the room with an easy grace that revealed his confidence and captivated me.

"You are a delightful woman, my lovely Esther," he said, leaning against the mantle, thumbs tucked into his belt. "I will see you again."

"It would be my pleasure, Your Majesty."

A chamberlain came for me and escorted me to new quarters. As we walked down a hallway where I had never been before, I wondered if it was possible that I could be in love after only one encounter with this strange and fascinating man. I felt like this must be love, but it was not the slow kind of knowing someone that I always thought it would be. And what about the king, I wondered. Had Ahasuerus been so charming with all of the other young women he had been with over the last weeks and months? Had they fallen in love with him too, or was what I had something special . . . different in some way from the others?

Verses from Solomon's Song coursed through my mind,

"Who is she who looks forth as the morning,
fair as the moon,
clear as the sun,
awesome as an army with banners?"

Dooste Man,

A week has passed since my night with the king, and I feel as though I am someone different than I was before that night. A feeling of fulfillment has soaked me the way a summer shower would run over me from my head to my toes, warm and wonderful. I remember the first time I went up on the roof all alone and stood with my arms raised to heaven as if that would allow me to absorb every drop that I could. It was as though the warm rain could cleanse me of all my worries and pain of the past, to free me to experience life at its fullest. But my time on the roof was nothing compared to this. I am a woman now, childish things have passed away, and new things have come.

One afternoon I took a long walk through my favorite garden and stopped at a fountain where angels' wings formed an arch. I swept my hand through the sparkling water and enjoyed the refreshing splashes. Leaning into the cool mist, I inhaled deeply trying to settle the anxious stirring within my chest.

A messenger wearing a red satin turban and tunic approached. Only the king's couriers dressed like that. My breath caught in my throat.

He spoke to Safiya first, "Madame, I have a message for your mistress." Stepping back, she gave him access to me as she smiled expectantly and searched me with wide eyes. Then turning to me, he said with a bow, "My lady, your servant Hathach told me where I could find you, and I apologize for disturbing you, but King Ahasuerus requests your presence this evening."

I swallowed before I could respond. "Yes, of course! Thank you."

"I will come for you at dusk," he said as he backed away with another bow.

A shiver ran through me, and my legs suddenly felt limp. Could it be? I wondered, lowering myself to the edge of the fountain where the cool mist gave me a chill. After a few moments, I rose and hurried to my apartment with Safiya. The king had not forgotten me! Thank you, Jehovah! Thank you!

Dusk approached like silver sheaves, and I was ushered into the presence of the king. As soon as he saw me, King Ahasuerus whisked me into his arms and kissed me. His hands on my back were strong and comforting. "I have thought of no one but you since the night we met," he said. "Tonight is ours."

A passion rose in me like I had never known before and I responded to his touch as though I had been created for this moment—all other aspirations and dreams drifted away like mist evaporating into a desert breeze.

I don't remember the meal we shared that night, but the king left an indelible imprint on my mind and heart. Gazing intently at me, a smile formed on his lips as fine lines appeared at the corners of his eyes. He said, taking my hand, "Esther, I love you more than anyone in this world for you are more beautiful than any woman I have beheld. I want you at my side as queen."

Leaning into him, I kissed him before I spoke. "It is an honor and my pleasure, Your Majesty."

Chapter 8

I ASKED MYSELF REPEATEDLY, "COULD THIS REALLY BE HAPPENING TO me?" When no assurance came, I asked Hegai. Hearing it from him would seal it in my reality. No, it was not a dream.

"Now others will bow prostrate before you," he said, "and give you the respect you deserve." He took my hand in both of his. "King Ahasuerus is planning a special banquet in your honor, Esther's Banquet, and has decreed a month-long celebration throughout the entire Persian Empire beginning on the day you are wed."

Dooste Man,

The maids chattered incessantly as they prepared to move me into the largest, most luxurious apartment in the entire harem.

Safiya's hands trembled as she tended to me. Hegai came to see me and glowed with a smile that was brighter than the morning sun. I am grateful to him for all his special attention, but I have to say goodbye to him since his duties to me have ended and I will probably never see him again. My life has been a series of "good-byes," but this time, rather than grief, I have something wonderful to look forward to.

I wonder what my parents would have thought of such a thing—their daughter, a queen! I believe they, too, would have been delighted in this extraordinary privilege given to me.

My prayer is this . . . "Lord, Jehovah, what is a Jewish woman to do as queen of such a great empire as Persia? Please help me to be a good and honorable queen and to perform my duties faithfully while still honoring You."

I did not have to tell my cousin the good news. The word of my selection as queen spread across Susa like the sun rising on the horizon. I sent for him to come to the Citadel and waited impatiently, bursting with joy. Finally, I saw Mordecai coming across the courtyard. He wore a colorful, striped tunic and a turban the color of ripe limes. His sash waved like a flag behind him, sandals flapping with his hurried steps. When he came close, he stopped and bowed to me.

"What are you doing, Mordecai?" I said.

He straightened and smiled, his eyes moist with tears.

"You must get used to this my dear Esther," he said. "You are to be honored above all women in Persia. This has come about for a particular purpose—for something great. Some day you will know why you are the chosen one. This cannot be a coincidence."

Safiya had been standing near me, far enough that she could not hear our conversations, but close enough to attend me if I needed her. When my cousin left to return home, Safiya and I returned to the harem.

"My lady," Safiya said. "Who is the older gentleman who visits you? Is he a relative?"

Her question was not a surprise. I knew it would come one day and had pondered how I would respond without lying, yet concealing my heritage.

"The man adopted me when my parents died. He had been a close friend and neighbor for many years, and since he had no children of his own, he graciously took me in. That was a long time ago. I came to love him like a father."

Safiya nodded as a wrinkle formed between her eyebrows, but she asked no more questions about him at that time.

Dooste man,

Cousin Mordecai told me that Tavita is expecting a child and, of course, she and Asher are overjoyed. At first I couldn't speak and tears welled up in my eyes. I recalled the excitement I felt when I contemplated having a family with Asher. I know I should feel happy for them, but in time I suppose that will come because I love Tavi and want to share in her happiness without feelings of regret. It's wrong that I feel this way! I know that, so why is my heart heavy?

I know that Jehovah's desire for me is to be the wife of a king and not of a silversmith, though I do not understand why. I remember one day as children when we played in Tavi's mother's shop. Tavi wrapped me in purple satin and put a mesh veil over my head and face. Then she bowed down to me and said in a deep voice, "Oh great and glorious one, I beg you to allow me to wash your feet." How silly we were then. Now look at us—Tavi makes dresses for others and I have become a queen—yet I am no more worthy than she is to receive this honor.

On the day of our wedding, I stood on the terrace overlooking the courtyard as droves of courtiers, princes, ambassadors and kings from every country arrived to celebrate the wedding and coronation. Hathach estimated that about ten thousand people came to Susa that week. At times, I felt as though I was living someone else's life, that all this could not be happening to an orphaned Jewish girl, but by some strange twist of fate, I stood where another was meant to be. If it had not been for Mordecai's reminders that my life was determined not by fate nor the position of the stars, but by our creator God's plan, I would have been delirious with fear of being found an imposter.

The time came for the long procession through the Citadel complex ending at the Throne Hall. Singers and musicians performed "Song of Heavens" and other classical pieces. The Throne Hall's ceiling was made of cedar, and the marble columns were sixty feet high, glistening with gold. The enormity of the place made me think of what I was about to embrace as the queen of Persia. Hegai had prepared me for much that I would face, but I knew that ahead laid challenges I could not meet without the help of Jehovah.

Saying a silent prayer, I took the first step in my life as royalty as my attendants led me down the long aisle blanketed with flowers. The train of my gown flowed behind me with a sound like a gentle waterfall, and the veil covering my face was as a mist that would soon evaporate when I sat beside my husband, the king.

With my heart racing wildly, I walked on until I approached the elevated throne where he sat, his gaze taking in every part of me. He was dressed in a white robe with gold embroidery across his shoulders, and jewels inlaid along the edges to its hem. His gold crown glimmered with emeralds, diamonds and sapphires, making him look almost like a god, and his flowered wreath matched my own.

I bowed. Attendants held a silk shawl over our heads throughout the ceremony that included readings by the priest from the "Avesta."

A young ring bearer carried a purple pillow upon which was my crown and matching gold ring inlaid with rubies and emeralds. Ahasuerus took my hand and slid the ring on my trembling finger, then gently placed the crown upon my head. I took the larger ring and slipped it onto the king's finger, and then we each dipped a pinky finger in the cup of honey and fed it to the other to insure a sweet life together.

We took a few steps to the Sofreh-ye Aghd, a luxurious Cashmere spread of rich, gold embroidered fabric on which was a mirror. Traditionally, the first thing that the bridegroom would see in the mirror should be the reflection of his wife-to-be. Two candelabra symbolizing light and fire stood on each side of the mirror. Also on the spread sat a tray with seven multi-colored herbs and spices to ward off evil spells, flatbread with a blessing written on it, decorated eggs and almonds symbolizing fertility. A basket of pomegranates and apples, heavenly fruits, and a cup of rose water to perfume the air, had been placed on the spread among other objects representing sweetness, blessing, health and prosperity.

I turned to face the thousands of onlookers who prostrated themselves before us, until trumpeters blew with a sound that must have reached the heavens. The people rose and gave a deafening cheer.

The air was thick with the scent of flowers and spices. Food was abundant with luscious fruits, meats and rich pastries on silver platters. Wine flowed like water—the finest wines from the far corners of the earth, and guests drank from gold goblets, some shaped like animals. The king's generosity toward his guests was boundless—gifts of gold and silver, jewelry and all types of precious stones. I never dreamed of festivities such as this! And to think that all this was to honor me as the new queen of King Ahasuerus . . . Esther, an ordinary Jewish maid is now the queen of Persia!

In the days following my coronation, exploring the Citadel became an adventure to me—no longer did it seem like a prison. I loved spending time in a garden where a beautiful, rare Sissoo tree grew, brought here from Gandhara. Yellow deer, found only in Persia, wandered freely in the garden and ate from my hand. On a day when the king took a rest from his official business, we strolled hand-in-hand as he spoke about some of the journeys he has taken.

"I have traveled throughout Persia, Queen Esther." He faced me and smiled. "And I have seen herds of gazelles, red deer, and lynxes. On the edge of a desert, I once saw an onager." A pair of mourning doves flew past us and perched on the birdbath. "Since the weather is more tolerable in Persepolis during the summer, I will take you, my dove, from Susa and go to the palace there which my father, King Darius, built. It is even more luxurious than here in Susa." His arm extended in a semi-circle in front of him. "You will like the gardens, fountains and tree-lined canals there, and perhaps on our way we will see some of the creatures I have told you about."

"I know I will enjoy that," I said, "since I have seen the animals you speak of only in paintings or carved on reliefs and clay pottery."

Dooste man,

Today, King Ahasuerus wanted me to accompany him to the temple of the goddess Ishtar Narundi. The idol was twice as tall as a human and adorned with a tiara sparkling with diamonds, emeralds and other precious stones. Huge carved lions crouched protectively at her feet. But what can these statues do?

We knelt in front of the statue and the king offered incense to it. My body bowed to Narundi, but my heart and mind bowed to the God of the Universe. Can idols deliver a nation from its enemies the way Jehovah does? Can a statue forgive sins the way my God does? The prophet Jeremiah spoke about idol worshippers who "Have eyes, but don't see, and have ears, but don't hear." I thank my Lord that I know the one, *true God and do not put my trust in false gods like the Persians do. As I watched the king kneeling, paying homage to the lifeless idol, I prayed that he would someday understand his error and worship the only living God.*

As queen, I had many privileges and among them was the honor to accompany the king at Council Hall. There came before him business matters from the Empire and beyond, and this gave me some understanding of the enormity of my husband's responsibilities. One day, satraps came with a report from the land of Judah. First, they remarked on the ease of travel, having used the Royal Road across the country. My heart raced wildly as I listened to a scribe read a letter from the rulers there. I had to check myself to avoid being overly interested. "We fear that the Jews will rebel against the king once they rebuild the City of Jerusalem and its walls," he read. "In order to protect the interests of the Great King Ahasuerus, it is necessary for the king," here his voice rose and deepened, "to give the command to make these men stop their rebuilding efforts." He bent down on one knee, extending his hand to the king as he continued. "The united plea of the satraps to Your Highness is to protect your interests by forbidding them to lay another brick in that cursed city." The scribe's words were as sharp as if a sword had passed through me.

Praying silently to Jehovah, I begged the Lord to put it in the king's heart to refuse their request.

"Leave them alone," King Ahasuerus ordered. "Many years ago, the great King Cyrus gave the Jews permission to return to their land and rebuild their cities. He even provided materials for the work, so who am I to reverse his decision? I will not grant their request."

Bowing before the king, the messengers backed away, then turned and left the court. Tears blurred my eyes as I thanked Jehovah for this miracle. I asked the king's permission to return to my apartment because suddenly, I had the desire to get out my long-forgotten chronicles and read over the notes I had written to my "Friend."

Chapter 9

Dooste Man,

It has been such a long time since I have written in this scroll. Four years have passed since my coronation, and my days and nights are filled with activities. I continually entertain ambassadors' wives, queens and their courts from other nations, and tour throughout Persia when the weather is nice. I enjoy entertaining the king's guests, but in the midst of so much busyness, I often feel alone. Oh, I realize it is an honor to be queen of this vast empire, but still my life seems empty. Perhaps the reason I am here is to pray for the king to have wisdom and discernment, which I do faithfully.

Cousin was always a great encouragement to me and often reminded me to be faithful in my heart to Jehovah in spite of what I must do physically. I told him that many dignitaries have invited me to attend their mountaintop shrines, but I went only when the king requested my presence. At Persian worship ceremonies, the leaders read from the Avesta, the sacred writings on religious doctrines and customs. Some of the doctrines seemed foolish to me, but since the Persians value truth above all other virtues, many of them have the same principles as my faith. One passage from the Avesta reminded me of a proverb of King Solomon's that I learned as a child.

"Let not mercy and truth forsake you;
Bind them around your neck.
Write them on the tablet of your heart,
And so find favor and high esteem
In the sight of God and man."

In the temple stood gold statues of men carrying goats as offerings to the gods, and there were lovely alabaster statuettes of rams and an ibex. When leaving the temple, I noticed an officer of the king's court called Haman. People bowed to him as he rode by on his horse, demanding homage as if he were a god or the king himself. His clothes stretched so tightly across his stomach that it appeared he would burst, spraying his entrails everywhere. He was taller than most men were and had piercing, black eyes, and a chin that slid down into his collar. I had heard of this man from Mordecai, and even though the king had commanded it, my cousin refused to bow down to Haman the way others did.

"I will never bow to that arrogant man." Mordecai said. "There is vengeance and hatred in his heart. I watched as he kicked a man to death because the man's mule ran amuck. No one dared stop him!" His face was redder than I had ever seen it, and his voice was almost a growl. It frightened me, but he continued. "Haman is full of evil and has no spark of light in him. I would rather die than bow to him."

I hoped and prayed that that would not be the case—to lose his life over a worthless human being.

Haman lived within the Citadel complex in a luxurious house with fountains and a lovely garden. People said that he was the wealthiest man in the empire next to the king, but Cousin said that all Haman's money was worth nothing because his heart was black and wicked. In the city, his sons also were known for their depravity because they beat other boys and robbed shopkeepers at the bazaar, but no one would stand up against them because of fear of their father.

One night as I joined the king in entertaining guests from Egypt, a servant hurried in to see me with an urgent message from Mordecai. He said that my cousin had overheard two of the palace guards plotting the king's assassination for that very night. A chill crept through my body as I listened, and for a moment, I could not speak. Turning to look at King Ahasuerus, he immediately noticed my distress.

"Esther, is something wrong? What is upsetting you?"

"Your Majesty, my—my lord. I—I need to speak to you privately, if you please. It's urgent," I said.

Getting up from his couch, the king said to his guests, "Please excuse me for a few minutes and continue to eat and drink as you wish. The servants will attend to you until I return."

He came to my seat and took my hand to help me up. My legs were shaking. We left the dining hall and walked onto a terrace before either of us spoke.

"What's troubling you, my lovely queen? I will punish the servant who caused you such distress. What is it?"

"No, Your Majesty, my king. You must not punish him. One of your trustworthy subjects has overhead Bigthan and Teresh, two of your doorkeepers, plotting to kill you. They plan to do it tonight."

The king's eyes narrowed and his jaw tightened.

"Who told you this?" he asked me.

"Your servant Mordecai has sent word to me by way of his messenger, Your Majesty. He is an honest man, upright and completely trustworthy. He would not lie to me on this matter or any other."

Calling the guards, in a voice that rattled the glasses in the dining hall, the king called out, "Guards! Arrest the doorkeepers Big and Ter immediately!"

Restraining his anger for a moment, he dismissed me. Within minutes, the captain returned and confirmed Mordecai's report. The king's voice thundered throughout the palace, startling everyone. Servants scurried this way and that to avoid falling under his wrath. The accused men were dragged from the palace and hung the same night.

Back at my apartment, I could not sleep, staying awake almost until dawn. I wished I could see my cousin and be comforted by him, remembering how he had held and rocked me when my parents died. Safiya brought me herbal tea and stayed by me until the blackness of night began to fade.

The next day, Safiya and I went to a secluded garden. I needed a quiet place, away from the noisy crowds. As I sat on a bench under the shade of a Sissoo tree, I noticed some flowers that I had never seen before.

"What are those delicate flowers, Safiya?"

"They are called *Isatis Aleppica*, my lady."

"I think they should be called 'teardrops,' because of the way their wispy, pale yellow petals hang like teardrops. Have they always been there?"

"I don't think so. The gardeners are always planting new flowers. It is beautiful here," Safiya said.

"And peaceful."

I heard others coming and turned around. It was King Ahasuerus and his servants. He reached out and took my hands.

"Esther, You were shaken last night. Have you recovered?"

"Yes. I am better today, my husband. Thank you."

With his one hand on the small of my back and the other holding my hand, he led me along the garden path, neither of us speaking. We strolled for a while, enjoying the sunshine and fragrances, and then walked back to the gate where our servants waited.

Dooste man,

Today Susa is quiet. There are more guards than usual in the streets and fewer people are moving about.

Safiya and I went to the inner garden again. I felt a solace there because it was more natural than the formal gardens throughout most of the Citadel complex. When I saw the "teardrop" flowers, I thought of the doorkeepers who were hanged. Safiya heard a rumor that the reason the men wanted to kill the king was because their daughters were taken away to become part of King Ahasuerus' harem in his most recently ordered gathering of virgins.

If that's the reason the men wanted to kill the king, I feel sorry for their families—they lost both their daughters and their husbands and will probably live in poverty the rest of their lives.

After a year had passed by since the assassination plot, I seldom saw the king. My maids and I walked through the gardens frequently, and Mordecai visited when he was permitted, but my life became very quiet. I wondered if King Ahasuerus was disappointed in me because I had not borne him a son, or perhaps he stopped calling for me because the new virgins had completed their time of preparation and were spending the evenings with him. I found it hard to understand why he needed so many women. With the hundreds of women in the harem who were just for him, he must have had a thousand children to call his own—but not a son from his queen. I prayed and prayed for Jehovah to bless me so the king would be delighted with me again, but so far, heaven was silent.

I had another great concern on my heart—that cousin of mine. I worried about him so much. After his last visit to the Citadel, Mordecai brought on another outburst from Haman. After frequent threats to my cousin for refusing to bow down when he passed, Haman complained to everyone in the court about taking care of that "dirty Jew Mordecai." I was relieved, but surprised, that Haman hadn't carried out his threats to my cousin, but what I didn't know at the time was that Haman was devising a plot to do away with not only Mordecai but also every Jew in the empire.

I did not understand why Mordecai would not give in and at least nod his head to the man. I knew that my cousin said he would worship only Jehovah, but I knelt when I had to go to the temples. I was not worshipping the idols, just giving outward homage to save my life and show obedience to the king. Why couldn't Cousin do the same and keep peace? Everyone knew that Haman was not someone to stand up against.

One night I woke up from my sleep with my heart racing and perspiration dripping from my face. In a dream, Haman rode on a huge black horse in the driving rain and chased down Cousin Mordecai who had been running away from him. Haman overtook him and trampled Cousin, leaving him for dead. I chased after them, screaming to Haman to stop. All of a sudden, it was quiet. The horse had disappeared, and Mordecai's body lay face down in the street. Vultures had already begun to tear at his flesh. Waving my arms frantically and screaming through tears at the birds, "Get away! Go!" I turned the body over, and it was not Cousin at all, but rather Haman who lay dead in a pool of blood.

Suddenly, I felt warm arms cradling me, and a soft, gentle hand stroking my head. I opened my eyes and saw the face of dear Safiya. She held me and wiped away my sweat and tears. Safiya rocked me until I stopped trembling, but I refused to allow myself to go back to sleep that night for fear the dream would return. The following morning it rained as if the dream had brought on a storm, and all day I could not shake off the feeling of dread.

Safiya brought me cinnamon tea that morning. Its aroma was delightful as I held the cup in both hands near my face and breathed in the scented steam.

"Please, Safiya, have some tea with me. Perhaps if we talk about something new it will take my mind off the nightmare. I know so little about you. Tell me, whom do you miss the most since you have come to serve in the harem."

Pouring herself tea in a delicate, gold-rimmed cup, Safiya sucked in her lower lip and hesitated for a long moment.

"Surely, my lady, you do not need to concern yourself about me. It's better not to think about such things."

"But Safiya, I would like to know you better. I think of you as a friend, not simply a servant. Are you sure you won't share a bit of your life with me?"

She stared into her teacup for a long moment and finally said, "I was in love with a man, but his family came between us because I was poor and my father could not offer a dowry. He tried to resist their influence because he also loved me." Her arms crossed her chest in a hug, then she shook her head slowly. "But his parents would not relent and forbade us to see each other."

"So much pride in our society. I'm sorry," I said.

Safiya continued. "To spare me further humiliation, my father decided to bring me here so that, even though unmarried, I would be provided for. I was the only girl in the family; the others were boys and had an advantage over me. I don't even know if they are married themselves now. Perhaps at least one of them is."

"What was his name, the man you loved, and where was he from?"

"His name is . . . was . . ." Safiya turned away as a torrent of tears flowed down her cheeks. "I am sorry, my lady. This is not a proper way for a maid to behave, but I must go."

Safiya ran from the room, her hands covering her face. I sat motionless, cup suspended. So we both have a secret sorrow, and my kindness toward her is not enough to fill the emptiness in her heart.

The following day, Hathach returned to the Citadel from running errands and I said, "Please tell me what is going on in the 'outside world' today. Is there anything exciting?"

He said, "Something terrible must have happened in the city, my lady. It seems the Jews are in mourning. They groan and sob, congregating in large clusters everywhere."

"Hathach, do you know which of them is Mordecai? He comes daily to the courtyard."

"Yes, my lady. He is now at the City Square near the king's gate. He is dressed in sackcloth and lay on his face weeping and wailing."

"Have you any idea what has distressed him so much? Has someone died?" I went to the terrace, but I could not see the area of the gate. Turning back to him, I said, "Please see if you can find out and take clean clothes to Mordecai. The guards will never allow him into the Citadel dressed like that, and I need to know what is happening."

Hathach hurried off and returned a short while later looking sullen. "The man Mordecai refused the clothes you offered, my lady."

Knowing something was seriously wrong, I felt helpless until I fell to my knees and prayed.

Later that day, Hathach returned with more news. "The Jews are in mourning because there is a royal decree offering to pay ten thousand talents of silver to anyone who annihilates the Jews. Haman will personally reward anyone who goes throughout the provinces slaying them during the month of Adar."

I gasped at hearing this and reached for a table to steady myself.

Hathach continued, "King Ahasuerus sealed the decree with his ring, making it irrevocable." Upon seeing my reaction, he said, "Why does this concern you so, my lady?"

Condemned to death! I slowly sank into a chair, my hands gripping the arms as if that could stop my trembling. Annihilated? Young and old, every man, woman and child. How could that be? How could the king allow such a thing?

My head had been spinning and leaning back, I closed my eyes. Yes, this too was a bad dream. In a while, I would wake up and the sun would be shining in a brilliant blue sky. After a few deep breaths, I slowly opened my eyes, expecting to find that this second nightmare had evaporated with the morning sun. However, it had not.

"Hathach please tell me it isn't true! This cannot be true."

"My lady, I'm sorry. It is true. I will have your maids attend to you, now. But before I go, would you like to send another message to Mordecai?"

"Please, see if you can find out how this has happened."

So many thoughts swam in my head. The Jews had faithfully served the king and contributed to the prosperity of Persia. In addition, a few years earlier, King Ahasuerus protected the right of the Jews to return to Jerusalem and rebuild the city. The edict just did not make sense.

Rashad came in and began brushing my hair. I wanted to give in to the soothing motion as she massaged my scalp, but it was impossible. Furat rubbed my feet with oil, the scent of which was nearly intoxicating, but the pounding in my head was incessant.

A while later, Hathach returned, entering my sitting room cautiously.

"My lady, the king's servant Haman is responsible for the edict. His hatred toward all the Jews, especially Mordecai, has consumed him because of Mordecai's refusal to honor him. Now Haman is determined to annihilate all of the Jewish people living in Persia."

He excused himself and left the room.

My maids stopped what they were doing and looked at me, confused, yet apparently reluctant to ask me any questions.

I went to my bedchamber alone and cried out in prayer, "Lord God Jehovah, could a man be as evil as this? Please spare your children from death. You, who saved us from the hand of Pharaoh and brought us out of Egypt, save Your people again from this threat of destruction. I beg You to defend us from the wrath of Haman who defiles Your name."

Dooste man,

Again, I suffer death. Again, I feel hopeless in the face of darkness. Moreover, like the rain pounding on the flowers in my garden bending their blossoms to the ground, I, too, am crushed. Where is God when his people despair because of this threat to our lives? I waited for an answer, but heaven was silent.

In their concern over me, my servants badger me with offers of a massage or tea and sweets, so I have dismissed them all. Today is not a day to think about beauty and food when the world has turned black like a starless, midnight sky.

Mordecai has commanded me to go to the king and plead with him to save our people, but how can I? It has been thirty days since the king has called for me, and Mordecai knows that I could lose my life for approaching the king without being summoned. He would spare me only if he is pleased to see me and extends his gold scepter, but I am so frightened. I cannot do what Mordecai has asked. I just cannot. As Hathach has said, a law of the Medes and Persians cannot be revoked. There is nothing I can do. Without a miracle, we are doomed.

Cousin Mordecai sent another message to me through Hathach.

"My lady, Mordecai the Jew has instructed me to give you a message, but you may not wish to hear it. Shall I say that you will not receive it?"

I was puzzled at his words and fearful. I nodded to him. "Please. What does he say?"

Hathach looked down as he spoke. "Mordecai says, 'Queen Esther, you must speak up for our people the Jews by using your influence with the king. Do not imagine that you in the king's palace can escape any more than the rest of us. For if you remain silent at this time, relief and deliverance will arise for the Jews from another place, and you and your father's house will perish.'"

I put my hand out to steady myself. Nevertheless, as I did, I knocked over the table beside me, sending the lamp careening across the floor. Hathach was quick and stomped on the flame before it had a chance to ignite the curtains. He pulled a chair over and helped me into it. Safiya fanned me as perspiration dripped from every pore in my body.

Approaching warily, Hathach spoke again, so quietly that I could barely hear him.

"Mordecai also says, 'Who knows whether you have not attained royalty for such a time as this?'"

Suddenly, sharp pains pierced my stomach. With my head in one hand and the other hand rubbing my stomach, I rocked in a vain attempt to soothe my body and soul.

Why had Mordecai put this responsibility on me? Surely, there was someone courageous enough to intervene on behalf of the people.

One minute I had confidence in Jehovah to deliver us, and the next minute my mind was tormented with fear and confusion. If Mordecai was right that I would die either way, I needed to get on my knees and ask for courage. Would God answer? Could I recognize His voice? I did not know, but I knelt and prayed that Jehovah would deliver us from Haman and to fill the king's heart with mercy for us.

There was no rest for me that night, and Safiya stayed close by in case I needed anything. I sat in a chair. I paced. I lay down and tossed from side to side. The pounding in my head was incessant.

Eventually, the sun rose with a blaze of red, orange and gold, followed by a clear, brilliant, blue sky. I stood gazing out the window for a very long time. A cloud floated by and seemed to stop in the sky. It looked white at first, but as I studied it, there were pale shades of pink, orange and yellow—last traces of the sunrise reluctant to let go. I thought of Jehovah and thanked Him for the wonders of His creation. I questioned Him. How many more sunrises will I see? If we Jews are Your chosen people, then why are we so hated that others continually try to destroy us?

I turned from the window and surveyed my apartment. I had come a long way from the little girl playing "dress-up" with Tavita.

How was it that I became queen of Persia at this critical moment in time?

Lord, answer me! I prayed. Then Hathach's words came to my mind—words that I had forgotten in my moment of shock. "Mordecai also had said, 'Who knows whether you have not attained royalty for such a time as this?'" *For such a time as this.* The words were like a repetitious chant in my mind.

I finally knew what I had to do.

"Have Hathach come to me immediately," I said to Safiya.

"Yes, my lady." She turned and went out the door, returning within minutes followed by Hathach.

"How may I be of service, Queen Esther?"

"Please locate Cousin Mordecai and give him this message that he and every Jew in Susa must fast from food and water for three days. Then I will approach the king." Safiya looked at me in horror.

I had no idea what I would say to King Ahasuerus, but I had to trust Jehovah to give me strength and wisdom for what I needed to do.

"Please Safiya; bring in Rashad, Furat and the other maids."

She hurried out, then returned shortly followed by the other maids.

"My dear servants and friends, I am a Jew."

They shrieked in disbelief, "No you cannot be! Surely you tease us!"

Quietly, but firmly, I said, "I am a Jew, and I believe my Lord Jehovah can overthrow this plan for our destruction."

They clutched one another's hands and all of them had tears in their eyes. Even as I spoke reassuring words to them, I was trying to convince myself, too. One minute I trusted, and the next minute I was fearful again. In my mind, I knew that if Jehovah did not answer our prayers for deliverance, I would spend eternity in heaven, but I did not want to face death at the hands of Haman.

As a surge of faith filled my heart, I told the maids that if Jehovah had held back the Red Sea to save us from the Egyptians centuries ago, He could save His people now, just as well. They nodded.

"Every Jew in Persia will fast and pray for three days and trust that Jehovah will give me favor as I intercede for them with King Ahasuerus."

The seriousness in their eyes showed me that they were thinking carefully about all I had said. Then Furat spoke first.

"I will fast with you, Queen Esther."

"As will I," Safiya and Rashad said in unison.

Safiya continued, "We will help you to bear this burden, but do you think that your God will also hear our prayers?"

"Oh, yes! How could He not hear you when you come to Him on behalf of His chosen people?"

Chapter 10

Dooste man,

My head is swimming with confusion. This morning, Cousin Mordecai received a great honor from King Ahasuerus. Does the king realize this is a man whom he has just condemned to death? And now to honor him? How can this be?

Hathach said that last night when the king was unable to sleep, a scribe read to him from the chronicles. When he came to the part about Mordecai saving the king's life from assassins, he realized that nothing had been done to reward Mordecai's loyalty. So today, the king's servants put a royal robe on him and honored him in a procession throughout the streets of Susa as he rode on the king's horse. The strangest part of all is that Haman, who hates my cousin vehemently, led the horse, while calling out, "Thus will it be done for the man whom the king delights to honor." This time people bowed to my cousin rather than to Haman.

I could only guess how this must have incensed Haman, and proves to me that the king did not realize that it is our people he has sentenced to death.

The first day of our fast, I did not even feel the hunger because I spent most of the day sleeping and praying. Rain beating on the roof all day and night added to the heaviness I felt.

The next day the sun returned. After the maids had completed their chores, I brought them all together and told them more about the Lord Jehovah. "He is one God and not one of many gods."

Furat asked, "How could one God be in charge of the entire universe when each of our gods controls one particular thing, such as warfare, harvest or fertility?"

As she and Rashad sat at my feet, I told them. "I worship only Jehovah because He created all things: the sun, moon, stars, trees, plants, and animals. His final creation was man and woman. He gave us this beautiful world to live in, and He loves us."

They had difficulty understanding that at one time the universe was all darkness until Jehovah made light, creating the sun to separate day and night and to give us the seasons. Their gazes never left my face as I spoke about the formation of the stars in the sky. "One day," I said, "a special star will shine as a sign to the world that the Messiah has come to earth to deliver His people from bondage and establish His kingdom—one greater than the Persian Empire."

Safiya asked, "If that is so, then why were your people conquered by so many nations?"

"Because of disobedience. Jehovah loves His people, but He also disciplines us when we turn our backs on Him."

Rashad said, "My lady, it seems that your people need their Messiah now that you again face destruction. Why does He wait?"

"I don't know, Rashad. I don't understand." Talking freely about my God encouraged me and gave me renewed physical strength.

As the next day wore on, every time my stomach rumbled, begging for food, I offered a prayer for mercy and compassion.

The third day of fasting arrived—the day I would attempt to approach the king. Safiya and I were solemn as she helped me on with my purple robe and crown. I gave her a long look before turning to leave. I held my head high, as Hegai had taught me years ago, and took the long walk to the entrance of the Throne Hall. Step by step, it seemed to take forever, with only the sound of my heart pounding in my ears. I felt a hot flush sweep over me as I wondered if this would be my last day on earth.

There was the king in deep conversation with several advisors. His throne stood high above the others. One by one, the men began to notice me until finally Ahasuerus also turned toward the doorway where I stood trembling. He looked surprised and stopped talking, then smiled and extended his scepter toward me, giving permission for me to enter. With a deep sigh, I bowed and walked to him, relieved that at least for now, he would allow me to live.

You can do this, Esther. You can do this . . . step . . . step . . . . The people are praying. I finally reached his throne. I bowed again, and gathered all the strength I could to rise and greet him with a smile. His pleasure at seeing me was apparent as he said, "What is it that you want, Esther? No matter what your request is, I will grant it—even if your wish is for half the kingdom. Now tell me, what is it you would like?"

"My desire, Your Majesty, is for you and your servant—Haman," I could hardly force his name out, "to come today to a banquet that I will prepare for you."

He looked at me with a half smile, eyebrows merging and his head cocked.

"Haman also?" He turned to look at him. "Haman, you must forgo any plans you have for this evening. The queen requests your presence at a feast."

I did not look at Haman, but kept my eyes on the king, then I let out a deep sigh. "Thank you, Your Majesty. I will go and prepare for you." I bowed and left the Throne Hall, this time with quick steps.

Dooste Man,

All the way back to my apartment tonight, I was praising Jehovah for sparing my life—at least for now, and I prayed that He would give me the courage I needed to speak up for my people.

I busied myself with dinner plans and had the banquet table set with polished bronze bowls, serving dishes of gold-plated silver, crafted in the shape of a winged ibex, and gold vases with fragrant roses.

The chef had been most helpful in suggesting a favorite meal of the king's— Charest made of chicken with ground walnuts, onions, and pomegranate juice. He had a servant bring the finest wine in the palace and baked spelt to dip in olive oil with spices.

Once I was satisfied that everything was in order, I tried to relax as Safiya touched up my make-up and hair, and waited for the arrival of King Ahasuerus and my enemy Haman.

Throughout the meal, it was difficult to restrain my hatred toward Haman, but I knew it was not the time to reveal my true feelings so I pretended to be interested in Haman's boasting about himself and his sons while stuffing bits of chicken into his cavernous mouth.

"Oh, they are bright and adventurous," he mumbled through his food. "Surely my sons are destined for great things."

I smiled weakly and nodded, but the king replied, "If they are as dedicated as you are, Haman, they will surely follow in your footsteps and become great in the Empire."

At that, I began to feel nauseous, but the king turned to me and said in a whisper, "I made a wise choice in selecting you, Esther. You are still the loveliest woman I have ever seen."

He took my cold hand in his warm one and looked intently at me. I could feel the heat rising up my neck and face, oblivious momentarily to our dinner guest. I could not help smiling as I looked into the king's shining, mischievous black eyes.

"Thank you, my husband."

Haman continued talking during this interlude between the king and me, and he never stopped stuffing his face until all the platters were empty. As he held up his goblet to the servant to be refilled, I could almost see his double chin developing another fold.

Again, the king asked me what I wanted from him, but I could not bring myself to say what was on my heart. I closed my eyes and inhaled slowly.

"I would be honored if Your Majesty and Haman would join me again for a banquet tomorrow evening."

Haman's eyes danced with delight at my request, and the king said, "Surely we will come." Then nodding toward Haman, he said, "I think our guest is still hungry. His appetite is insatiable."

Haman smiled, still gnawing on a chicken leg. He dropped it with a clunk onto his plate and hastily wiped his hands on a napkin letting it fall to the floor.

I forced a smile though I felt like vomiting. "Thank you, my lord. I would be pleased to have you come."

"Certainly not as pleased as I shall be," Haman said. His broad smile exposed the remains of his meal stuck between his teeth. We rose from the table. The king cupped my face in his hands and kissed my lips. "Until tomorrow," he said, and left with his servants and chief advisor. His kisses always made me want to melt into his arms, but tonight all I could feel was a sense of shame for not following through with my plan.

When I was finally alone, I leaned my back against the door and closed my eyes. I have let them down. Mordecai, Aunt Mehry, Tavita and every one of my fellowmen . . . and my Lord Jehovah! I blew out a long, deep breath, and then took my parchment from its hiding place.

Dooste man,

How could I have been so cowardly? For now, I must face this man again. Why wasn't I able to say what I needed to say? Tomorrow I must be prepared to speak out the truth. Jehovah, please, give me the right words. Otherwise, I cannot do this thing without You.

The following day I sipped heated rose water to help ease my stomach pain. A hot, lavender scented bath helped soothe me before the king and Haman arrived.

That evening we ate fish seasoned with mint and ground sesame, but even such a delicacy was not enough to settle the churning in my stomach.

After we finished our meal, the king said to me, "No more games, my darling Esther. Surely tonight you will tell me what is on your mind. What could it be? Ask me for anything you like."

His gaze was disarming, but I could not allow myself to be distracted. I wavered only a second. Then, gathering my courage, I sat erect and looked hard at him.

"Your Majesty, my husband, I ask that you spare my life and the lives of my people, the Jews."

He leaned toward me, eyebrows pulled together, then shook his head slowly and looked deeply into my eyes.

"Esther, my love, your life has never been in jeopardy. What do you mean by this strange request?"

Taking his hands in mine, I took a huge breath and said, "My lord, I am a Jewess and according to an edict that bears your seal, we have been marked for annihilation, to be massacred." My throat constricted, but I forced myself to continue. "That edict also promises a reward to those who murder us."

"You must be mistaken, my darling Esther," said Ahasuerus, kissing my fingertips. "No one wishes to harm you."

I shook my head. "My lord, I would not have spoken up if we had only been sold into slavery, but we are condemned to death. All of my people!"

Suddenly Haman choked, spraying half-chewed food across the table. Clasping his throat, his eyes bulged as he shrank back.

The king looked at him and then turned back to me with confusion. "Who would presume to do this thing you speak of, to plan this treachery?"

Springing to my feet, I pointed, and suddenly all the anger and grief of the last four days fueled my rage. "Your enemy and mine is the man who sits at this table—the wicked Haman! It is he who has put a price on my head and my people!"

Ahasuerus rose with the ferocity of a lion and turned toward Haman, who was now cowering behind a bewildered servant. The king bellowed, "Haman? How could this be? What have you done?"

The king rushed from the dining room, out the door and into the garden. As he did, Haman, with eyes blazing, lunged at me, sending a shiver of panic through me.

"No! Get away," I screamed as I held my hands out to push him off.

Haman groveled as he grasped my legs.

"Have mercy on me! Mercy! I didn't know you were one of them."

At that moment, the king reentered the room followed by a dozen guards and saw Haman clinging to me, His voice thundered, "What! Now you intend to molest my queen?"

Haman's body recoiled into a tight ball as he shrieked. Unearthly screams spewed from him as the guards pinned him to the ground.

I ran to the king and clutched him, like a child after a nightmare. His strong arms wrapped around me as I buried my face in his pounding chest.

"Guards," he said, almost in a whisper. "Remove my ring from his hand and hang him."

Haman howled when the captain of the guards yanked the ring from him and the guards threw a hood over his head. They dragged him away while he continued to kick and writhe. "There is a gallows already built in Haman's courtyard," the captain said, "one on which he had planned to hang Mordecai the Jew. Take him there!"

I closed my eyes, but I could hear Haman's muffled cries like a pig being slaughtered.

The king stroked my head and kissed my wet cheeks. We stood that way until my sobbing subsided. I could barely hear him when he said, "How did I allow this to happen? I trusted him. My dearest love, I trusted him even with your life."

Without another word, he gently took my hand and led me to his bedchamber, and he held me close and loved me until the fear left, the way a stillness returns after a storm. For a long time I did not want to let go of him, nor it seemed, he of me.

Dooste man,

Though Haman is dead, we Jews are still a condemned people. Under the law of the Medes and Persians, the edict can never be revoked . . . not even by the king. Therefore, the order to annihilate us still stands. On the thirteenth day of Adar, eleven months from now, the law states that we are to die.

The king assured me that somehow, he would find a way to protect us, but his advisors have been unable to determine how that could be. They said it could not be done.

I refuse to accept this . . . Mordecai refuses to accept this. He said that if Jehovah has saved us until now, He would not allow the annihilation to take place. We are praying for an answer.

The king permitted me to celebrate Shabbat with Mordecai and a few others. The first time we did this in the palace, the Lord's anointing fell on Mordecai in such a powerful way that we stood in awe for hours, and then sang songs of praise until our voices were hoarse.

Late afternoon before a Shabbat, I found some peace in being able to speak openly of my Lord Jehovah to Safiya and Rashad as we strolled in a garden. Canaries flew by us in graceful arcs as they serenaded us. I sat on a bench and the women sat in the grass at my feet.

"This is not the first time our enemies have tried to destroy my people. Many years ago, Jehovah delivered Moses and the Jewish nation from annihilation by the Egyptians. He sent plagues on them—frogs and locusts—"

The maids gasped. "How disgusting!"

"Yes, it must have been. But that was not the worst plague. The last and most terrible was the plague of death."

Their eyes widened in fear as they leaned in closer.

"Jehovah sent an Angel of Death throughout Egypt and killed the firstborn of every man and animal. The weeping and wailing continued for days, and not one family escaped without loss of life except in the Jewish households."

"How could that be?" Safiya asked.

"The Lord had instructed every Jewish family to kill and eat a lamb, and to spread its blood over their door. Wherever the Death Angel saw the blood, he passed by that home."

"That's strange," said Rashad. "Blood over the door?"

"Yes. In the Jewish faith, blood is always a symbol of protection and a vital part of worship as a sacrifice for sin. Every year we remember the time of Passover."

They seemed to be in deep thought as we walked back inside since Mordecai would be waiting for me.

The following day after my mid-day meal, Safiya said, "Would you tell us another story about the ways your God saved you? I want to believe that He will save you now also." There seemed to be a tear in the corner of her eye.

"I would be pleased to speak of that. It also increases my hope for His deliverance." Sitting down on a couch, I motioned to her and Rashad to sit beside me. They shook their heads and sat at my feet, smoothing their skirts around them.

"Have you heard of the city of Jericho?" I asked.

"No," they said in unison.

"It was a large, walled city near the Jordan River," I said. "The Jews destroyed it about one-thousand years ago, and it has never been rebuilt. The Commander called down a curse on any builder who would lay the foundation or put up the gates. No one ever dared to go against the God who performs miracles."

Safiya asked, "How did the city fall? Was that a miracle?"

"Yes. It was amazing! Jericho was the first city the Jewish nation conquered after they fled Egypt. An angel appeared to the leader Joshua and gave them strange instructions as to how they would take the city."

Rashad tipped her head and asked, "Don't armies just attack a city with spears, swords and arrows after they break through the gates?"

"Yes, but the miracle was that the Jews didn't have to tear down the walls. Jehovah made them fall in a miraculous way. Only the sound of trumpets and the people's yelling—and, most importantly, the Lord's power—brought down the walls so the Lord's army could rush in and destroy everything."

"With trumpets and shouting?" asked Safiya. "Destroyed everything? Didn't they take prisoners?"

"None survived except for one family. A prostitute's family was rescued because previously she had helped Jewish spies to escape the city."

Rashad and Safiya looked at each other at the word "prostitute," apparently surprised to hear it from my lips.

Twisting a towel in her hands, Safiya said. "Will your God do something mystical this time?"

I shrugged and shook my head. "I don't know what He will do, but I must admit that I am impatient. I do not want the blood of my people to cover this land."

I turned away from them to hide the tears spilling from my eyes and pressed my lips together. After a long pause, I answered. "We will have to wait and see. We will wait and see."

When I was alone, I struggled with doubt. What if we were still under Jehovah's wrath? He punished us by causing us to be defeated by the Babylonians. Has He forgiven us? Do we now have His favor?

I sat and prayed, rocking, "Lord Jehovah, please forgive Your people for our unfaithfulness, for forgetting You and failing to honor Your holy days and Your laws. Please forgive us and restore us by Your great mercy."

Chapter 11

Since Haman and his sons were dead, the king took over their property and gave me the estate as gift. King Ahasuerus asked me if I knew anyone who could oversee it, so I recommended Cousin Mordecai and told the king about my relationship with him. The king remembered honoring Mordecai for saving his life and was pleased to give him more responsibility.

The Council Hall brimmed with activity while the king summoned my cousin who arrived hurriedly, cheeks flushed and his robe flapping behind him.

As my cousin knelt before the throne, the king said, "My servant Mordecai, you have proven that you are a loyal servant and one to be trusted." The king held out his hand toward Mordecai. "In addition to the management of Haman's estate, I give you this ring with all the authority that brings with it, and appoint you as Prime Minister of this great land."

The king slid the gold, embossed ring onto Mordecai's finger, and all the court officials, attendants and visitors cheered at the wonderful honor that the king bestowed on him. Cousin Mordecai worked hard for the welfare of our people and his reputation spread throughout the empire. He was honored by all, second only to the king.

But in spite of Mordecai's appointment, we Jews still lived in fear of annihilation. Nearly two and a half months had passed since Haman's death. The days were long and the nights were filled with dread as each day brought us nearer to fatality. When I spent time with the king, it was hard to pretend I was happy. Fearing to bring it up again, I thought perhaps he had forgotten the dreadful edict. Until finally one evening, King Ahasuerus sent for me, and after one of the most elegant meals we had shared together, while he sipped his wine, I fell in a heap before him, weeping bitterly.

"Your Majesty," I begged him. "You must save my people whose lives are still at risk and somehow reverse the evil that Haman planned against us." My words were so jumbled; I could see through my tears that he could not understand me.

"Please! Please! You must reverse this evil plan of Haman." Rising to my feet with a new boldness, strength came into my voice. "If it seems right to you, and you have not forgotten my people the Jews, you must do something to revoke the law written by Haman for our annihilation. Surely, you can! You are the king!"

He stood to face me with a softness in his eyes like grief, as if he looked at one dying. He said nothing until moments later when a spark of inspiration took hold of him.

"My dear Queen Esther, it is not in my power to revoke any laws previously written, you know that." Then, taking my hand, he said, "but I will give permission to Mordecai and you to write a new decree in my name allowing all Jews to protect their lives—to destroy the forces of any people who would try to assault you."

Turning from me, he turned to his servants. "Scribes!" he called. "Go to Mordecai and have him write a new edict, and have it translated into every language spoken in the kingdom so that no one will have an excuse to say they were not informed. My couriers must use the fastest horses to carry this message everywhere.

To Jews throughout the Empire of Persia, and to every governor, prince and official:

In the name of the great King Ahasuerus, it is hereby proclaimed that on the thirteenth day of Adar, in every province of Persia, permission is granted to every Jewish person to defend themselves from anyone attempting to assault them. The Jews may destroy their enemies and plunder their possessions.

The thirteenth day of Adar finally came bringing rivers of bloodshed in both the city and throughout the empire. In Susa alone, 500 people died trying to assault their Jewish neighbors. Hatred rampaged, fueled by either prejudice rooted in many generations, or the love of money—blood money. I was with the king at dinner when couriers arrived to report the number of deaths.

"Esther," Ahasuerus said, "is it enough, or is there something more that you wish to be done?"

My response was quick. "My lord, I ask that tomorrow also, the Jews in Susa could defend themselves against anyone who wanted to harm us. I also ask that the ten sons of Haman be hanged because they are worse than their father."

King Ahasuerus gave a command for these things to be done.

The following day, another 300 men were killed in Susa so that we could finally live in peace. The Jews killed 75,000 throughout all the provinces of Persia, yet they didn't take any of their possessions. I was sorry to know that so many people hated us, but I was glad that the king wanted to please me and that he had granted my wishes.

Dooste man,

Today there was a holiday with feasting throughout the city among the Jews and their friends. People are giving gifts to each other and giving food to the poor in honor of Jehovah's deliverance. I haven't been this happy for a long time. It's a relief to openly express my faith.

In time, Susa and the countryside resumed normal activities. The bazaars bustled with vendors and shoppers; caravans rode into the city with spices and exotic fruit from far off countries; and children played in fountains throughout the city.

As the new Prime Minister, Mordecai looked quite handsome wearing blue and white royal garments and a gold crown. He earned great respect, worked for the good of the people, and brought peace to all his countrymen because he was a just man.

He wrote another decree commanding all Jews to hold an annual celebration to remember our great deliverance. There was to be a time of fasting, followed by two days of feasting, on the fourteenth and fifteenth days of Adar. Gifts were to be exchanged among friends and relatives, and donations given to the poor. In this way our descendants would never forget what Jehovah did for us during the days of Ahasuerus, King of Persia.

Chapter 12

ONCE I HAD EXPERIENCED FREEDOM, MY HEART FELT HEAVY EACH TIME I looked at Safiya, who lived in a bondage of her own. Separated from her family and the man she loved, she pushed ahead, trying to forget her pain, yet she had made my life not only tolerable but also enjoyable as she served me. She seemed to read my moods and always knew what tea to bring me or what color gown I should wear to brighten my complexion. One day I asked Hathach to dispatch a servant to Safiya's family's home to inquire about them.

Hathach brought Behrooz, a trusted courier, to my apartment. The day was cool and crisp, a welcome relief after weeks of sultry weather. I paced across the carpet, avoiding the fringed edges and following the design of a young woman with flowing black hair. She seemed suspended above the ground with a pitcher in her hand, and an old man sat on the ground holding a cup upwards.

I felt entranced for a moment and then returned to the business at hand.

"Behrooz, you are to . . . discretely . . . inquire in the town of Tabriz about the family of PezhmAn. Also ask about the young man named Hafez."

"I am pleased to do your bidding, Your Majesty." He bowed and left immediately.

Two days later Hathach announced that his servant had returned. "I am sure you will be pleased with his report," he said smiling.

The courier entered looking flushed, perhaps from his short journey. His eyes glistened with excitement as he faced me and bowed on one knee, then rose.

"Your Majesty, the family of PezhmAn is poor but well respected in the community. Their home is plain but adequate, and they offered me food for my return journey, which I accepted."

I was impatient. "Yes, yes! And what about the young man Hafez?"

"Your Majesty, he is in good health and works as a carpenter, making a good living. He remains unmarried. A neighbor said he pines for a lost love."

I clasped my hands and closed my eyes, offering a prayer of thanks.

"Behrooz, you have done well and you shall be rewarded. Thank you."

He bowed, backed away, turned and left the room.

"Thank you, Hathach. I will speak to you about this matter on another day. For now, you are dismissed."

After they were gone, I stretched out on the couch and stared for a long time at the tiled ceiling and the elegant arches over the windows and doors. I thought of the great loss it would be to me to have Safiya leave my service and remembered how her sweet spirit comforted me when I was new to the harem. "An angel sent from Jehovah," I had thought back then.

As Safiya laid out my bedclothes later that night, I watched her moving gracefully, purposefully. Suddenly my heart felt gripped in a stranglehold. I gasped involuntarily.

She turned to me and said, "My lady! What is wrong? Are you in pain?"

She took my arm and led me to the couch. Rashad had heard Safiya's shock and came hurrying over with a glass of water.

"My lady, please drink. What is it?" She gently lifted my head with her hand and held the glass to my lips. I sipped.

"I'm sorry, Safiya, Rashad. I didn't mean to alarm you," I said. "I'm fine. I really am."

They looked at each other, and then back at me, shaking their heads. Obviously I had not fooled them. After I got into bed, they lingered longer than usual before extinguishing the lamps.

When I was sure they had gone, I gave into my grief and sobbed quietly as a war raged within my heart. I loved Safiya and needed her. She did not know about my inquiry regarding Hafez and probably thinks he has married by now. She has accepted her lot and seems satisfied. Then another voice broke into my thoughts, if you truly love her, you would let her go so that she will find happiness. Stop being selfish, Esther. Eventually, I fell asleep, but I was restless all night.

When I awoke in the morning, I went to the window and looked down into the garden. The sun shot streaks of pink and orange into the lightening sky and a few wispy clouds sailed along happily on a soft breeze. I inhaled the crisp, cool air and felt revitalized by it. As I exhaled slowly, it was as though the darkness in my selfish soul dissipated and wafted away on the breeze. I knew what I had to do, but first, I took out my scroll and removed the lid from my ink well, studying the intricate etchings of doves flying above treetops.

Like a canary caged
still sings its song
bringing joy to its hearers,
so the little maid serves with a smile
concealing wounds
overshadowing her heart.

Yearning to set it free
O open the door to the heavens.
Tentative it slides
sideways to the open space
tries its wings to perch on a cypress.
Then away!

I sent for Hathach in the morning as soon as I had dressed and eaten. "Please send Behrooz back to Tabriz and have him bring PezhmAn and Hafez here to the Citadel to meet with me tomorrow. Have them come to the king's garden so they are not seen by gossiping servants."

"As you wish," he said. "You are an exceptional woman, my queen."

The following day, when I had finished a wonderful meal of lamb with saffron rice and vegetables, Behrooz returned. Hathach ushered him in immediately.

"Your Majesty, the men you sent for await you in the king's garden."

My heart fluttered inside of me like a butterfly hovering over a strange flower. "Thank you," I said, rising from my couch.

I clutched my skirt in both hands as I hurried along the hallway and down the steps. Slow down, Esther. Don't get into a panic, I reminded myself. Hathach kept pace with me, seemingly as anxious as I was. I never noticed before how far it was to that exquisite garden where exotic birds nested in fruit trees and every imaginable flower bloomed almost year round. We finally arrived, and I sat down in a cushioned armchair and reached for a cup of mint tea. It would help to calm me. Taking several deep breaths, I inhaled slowly until the pounding of my heart subsided.

"Hathach," I said, "you may bring them in."

He bowed solemnly and then walked inside to a room where the two men waited and received instructions as to their conduct before royalty. Hathach returned moments later followed by two finely dressed gentlemen. The older shuffled nervously along the walk. I smiled.

"Your Majesty Queen Esther," said Hathach, "May I present to you PezhmAn, the father of Safiya your handmaid, and Hafez, as you requested."

The men bowed low, and then stood before me with quizzical expressions on their faces. I studied them both carefully, PezhmAn, in a stiff brown tunic, obviously being worn for the first time.

Hafez wore a white linen tunic with a purple sash around his waist and a matching turban. He was very handsome with sharp, angular cheekbones and jaw. He had a seriousness that belied his years. I turned my attention to the older man who stood rubbing his hands and shifting his weight from one foot to the other.

"PezhmAn," I said.

He bowed. "Your Majesty."

"You brought your daughter Safiya to serve here at the Citadel five years ago. She has proven to be faithful and diligent in all her work. You should be proud of raising such a lovely girl."

"Thank you, Your Majesty. That was my hope. It grieved me to send her away from home, but we had no choice."

Then turning to look at Hafez, I said, "Am I correct in that you wanted to marry PezhmAn's daughter, but your parents would not permit you to do so because there was no dowry?"

He folded his hands in front of him and bowed his head. "That is correct, Your Majesty."

I took a sip of tea before continuing. "I must ask a personal question. Hafez, do you still love PezhmAn's daughter Safiya, and have you been faithful in your heart to her these last years?"

"Against all hope, Your Majesty, I have loved no one else, and since the day her father brought her here to the Citadel, I have devoted myself only to my work."

That expression of love is what I so longed to hear from his lips. I sighed and closed my eyes for a moment before continuing.

"Hafez, would your parents permit your marriage to Safiya if her father were to provide a substantial dowry?"

"I believe that they would give their approval. Although with no disrespect, Your Majesty, that is not the case with PezhmAn since he is a poor man."

"Thank you, Hafez. That is what I needed to know. You are dismissed for now." I stretched my hand toward Behrooz. "Now go with my servant who will see to your needs."

Both men stepped back with a bow and turned to go. I turned to PezhmAn. "You are to remain here."

After Hafez left the garden, PezhmAn stood sheepishly, like a child before a harsh teacher.

Extending my hand to a chair next to me, I said, "Please sit down. "

He lowered himself into the chair, allowing a long sigh to escape. A servant offered him a glass of wine, which he accepted with a trembling hand. He raised it to his lips and sipped slowly.

"I have been told that you changed your name the day you brought your daughter to the Citadel," I said. "Why was that?"

With a quiet, shaky voice he replied, "Your Majesty, my name was Majid, meaning 'great and honorable,' but on that day, I told everyone to call me 'PezhmAn' because I was brokenhearted."

I blinked, trying to restrain the tears that began to fill my eyes. I sat silently for a moment.

"I regret that it was necessary for you to give up your daughter," I said finally, "but I am grateful to have had her service. She is a jewel. But now her service to me must end." I reached and took his hand. He drew back.

"Why?" he stammered. "Wh—what has happened?"

"I have spoken to King Ahasuerus about you, and today you will take back your true name, Majid." His mouth hung open in surprise. "You have been found honorable among your friends and neighbors in spite of great hardship and poverty. And because of your daughter Safiya, today your fortunes have turned." My heart quivered inside of me in anticipation. "The king has appointed you as assistant to the satrap in your province, and eventually you will take over that position and govern the province on behalf of the king."

Clearly stunned, Majid slid from his chair and knelt before me.

I continued, "In addition, a home has been provided for you and your family, as well as a sizeable dowry for your daughter, my friend, Safiya. I will miss her greatly."

Tears streamed down his face and into his beard. My own tears stung my eyes.

"For my daughter? You have done all this for my daughter's sake?"

I took his shaking hands to raise him and stood facing him. "Yes, Majid, Safiya has been an example to all of the maids for her kindness and meticulous service. Today I set her free to return to your family. All I ask in return is that she returns with her first child to visit me. I will have a gift for them both."

Majid bowed, and then wiped his face with the back of his hand. "Many thanks to a most gracious queen," he whispered.

I nodded and said to the servant who had returned, "Behrooz, please take Majid and provide him proper refreshment, then bring him to my apartment."

"Yes, Your Majesty." Behrooz bowed, and then led Majid to the men's quarters.

Chapter 13

HATHACH ACCOMPANIED ME BACK TO MY APARTMENT. "LET ME KNOW when the gentlemen are ready," I told him.

When he bowed, I noticed the corners of his mouth turned up slightly, and when he turned to go, a smile had spread across his face. *Many persons have been made happy today,* I thought.

Safiya entered carrying fluffy towels and bottles of soap, oil and perfume. With a curtsey she asked, "My lady, will you be having a bath this afternoon?"

"Yes, Safiya, but will you ask Furat and Rashad to prepare one also for you? Her mouth opened as if to speak and she looked at me as if I had turned into a ghost. "My lady, I . . . I . . . forgive me, please. I will have Furat and Rashad come in, but for . . . ?"

With a quiet laugh, I reached out to her and drew her into my arms. She stiffened.

"Wh—what?" she gasped. "My lady!"

"Safiya, this is a special day for you. You must look on the outside like the princess that you are inside. I will explain everything to you shortly. For now, you must bathe and dress in a formal gown. Rashad will help you with your hair."

Rashad entered the room and looked as puzzled as Safiya.

"Rashad," I said, "please assist Safiya to bathe and dress. Soon you will all know of Safiya's special blessing."

The maids did as they had been instructed, and when Safiya returned to my room, the sight of her was breathtaking. Furat's skill with make-up had transformed a maid into a princess. Her eyes sparkled. Her long, black hair was twisted upward and ornamented with pearls and small white flowers. Rashad had chosen a gown for Safiya of white chiffon with an emerald green satin sash and matching slippers. Only one thing was missing—her smile. Her eyebrows knit together and her lips pursed in confusion.

"My dear Safiya, you look lovely." I said, extending my hand toward the chair beside me, "Please sit down. And smile. Everything is fine—I promise you."

She lowered herself slowly, careful to smooth her dress around her. The corners of her lips had the slightest hint of a smile, but I knew that would change in a moment.

Our eyes turned toward the terrace where we could see someone's shadow pacing. I said to a servant, "Please tell our guest that he may come in now."

A soft breeze blew into the room as Hafez entered.

Safiya gasped, clutching the arms of her chair and leaned forward. "Father?" She turned from him to me, and then back again to her father.

He gazed at his daughter, now fully a woman, and shaking, ran to her with outstretched arms.

"Safiya, my child!" he cried. "My long lost child!"

Rising from her chair, Safiya put her hand to her mouth. "How could it be?"

Tears welled up in my eyes as I watched this reunion—a lost and lonely woman-child with her father. As they held each other, it seemed that they were unaware that anyone else was present.

Hathach grasped the handle of the door to my chambers and thrust it open. Hafez stood there, looking like a soldier lining up for a victory parade in the purple linen tunic and silk turban provided for him.

"Sir." Hathach stepped to one side and bowed. "You may come in now."

Hafez took a tentative step forward.

"Your Majesty the Queen," Hathach cleared his throat. "May I present to you the noble Hafez."

"Hafez," Safiya whispered his name as if she was addressing the king himself.

Safiya looked over her father's shoulder, and then stiffened like a statue, staring at Hafez as he walked toward her, his smile spanning the width of his face. "I have permission, Safiya, from your father and your mistress the queen to marry you if you will have me." He extended his right hand to her.

She stepped back from her father's embrace and looked at me. I was blotting my tears and murmured into my handkerchief, "Your young man is waiting for an answer."

"My lady," she said, "is this dream?" but she was already walking slowly toward Hafez, lifting her hand to take his. Time seemed to stand still as the two lovers met and joined hands, gazing into each other's eyes.

I felt as though I was intruding on sacred ground, reluctant to speak and possibly break the spell. "It is all true, my faithful friend Safiya." I rose to my full height and separated my folded hands in a gesture of openness. "I release you from my service this moment. You are free to take anything you like with you from the palace. But go now and live a long and happy life."

Hathach, Majid and I quietly left the room.

Dooste man,

One year has passed since the great deliverance, and I have felt as free as a gazelle on the open terrain since everyone knows I am a Jewess and I have nothing to hide. The king has given me permission to invite some of my friends to the palace for a big celebration, and I cannot wait to see dear Tavita again, for I will surely have her come. I have tried to imagine how her children look. Will they resemble her or Asher? And Aunt Mehry—I have missed her so.

Yesterday, all the Jews in Persia fasted as a reminder of our time of mourning and prayer to win our freedom. Mordecai referred to it as "Esther's Fast." Now, on the fourteenth day of Adar, we will celebrate throughout Persia as we commemorate the Feast of Purim for the first time. We chose this name because "pur" means, "chosen by lot" and that is how Haman determined the date for his attempted destruction of my people . . . a man that gambled to choose a day to kill.

In addition to the abundance of food, wine and gift-giving during Purim, we watched a drama of the story of our deliverance from Haman. Each time an actor mentioned Haman's name, everyone hissed and booed, and the king pounded the table.

He turned to me, laughing. "I may not be Jewish, but today I shall pretend that I am."

He watched me constantly with a glow in his eyes, as I rocked our new son in my arms. Ahasuerus, the bold leader of many nations, has a tender place in his heart for his little one and me. My prayer was that this child would, one day perhaps, sit on his father's throne and rule wisely.

Cousin Mordecai came to my place at the table and reached for the baby. He handed him to the nursemaid. His smile shone like the gold medallion he wore around his neck. "Queen Esther, there is someone here who would like to speak with you. May I bring her to you now?"

Looking over Mordecai's shoulder, I saw Tavita tentatively walking toward me. She was no longer a child as I remembered her, but a mature woman with a glow in her cheeks and a sparkle in her eyes. Her silk azure gown was lovely, and she had arranged her hair the way she had done mine that day in her mother's workroom so long ago. My heart beating wildly, I sprang and rushed toward her, forgetting the decorum befitting a queen.

"Tavita! My sister, my friend! Oh, how wonderful to see you!"

We laughed as we hugged each other, as a million inarticulate phrases blended together. Aunt Mehry stepped up and joined in the embrace. She cupped my face in her hands as she shook her head and whispered, "A queen—my Esther, a queen."

"Yes, dear aunt. Can you believe it?" I said.

"I can believe it, my dear one. I can believe it."

Asher stood off to the side, rubbing his hands. Behind him stood their oldest son who looked just like his father with curly, dark hair framing his face.

When Asher caught my eye, he dropped his hands to his side and bowed solemnly. His face twisted as he held back a smile. The little boy at his side copied his father's stiff bow.

I walked over to him. "Asher, my friend and brother!" I said, grasping his hands in mine. "It's wonderful to see you here with your family."

"Thank you, Your Highness. We are pleased to have been invited."

"It would not have been a proper celebration without you, Tavi and Aunt Mehry present."

The boy tugged on Asher's sleeve. "Father, do you think Uncle Mordecai would allow me to sit on his throne for just a minute?"

"Ask him and see," Asher told him.

"Oh, Father. Would you ask him for me?"

Asher smiled and nudged his son toward Mordecai. "You can do it, son."

Mordecai, always one to see a need, came to the boy's rescue.

"Asher! Do you think that son of yours would like to try out my favorite chair?"

"Oh, yes! Please!" the boy said. Then, embarrassed by his outburst, he dropped his eyes.

Mordecai reached out his hand to the boy. "It's all right. I think you will like it. It is big, but one day you will grow into it. Who knows? Perhaps one day you will be a Prime Minister. I can hear it now—'The new Prime Minister Asher, son of the silversmith!'"

Young Asher pulled himself up and beamed, settling into the huge chair. "I'll have my brother Daniel help me. Did you know we will be moving to Judah, uncle Mordecai?"

"Yes! We need young men such as yourself and your brother to help bring Jerusalem back to her former glory."

Tavita and I left the banquet room and found a quiet place in the garden to talk. There was a bench facing a pool where warblers fluttered and splashed. The scent of roses was intoxicating. "You look radiant, Tavita. Family life suits you well, my dear friend."

"Oh, I'm very happy, Esther—may I call you Esther, Your Highness?" She laughed slightly with her hand to her mouth. I nodded, still smiling. "At first my parents were reluctant to accept Asher's proposal—because of you." She looked down at her hands before continuing. "But finally they decided that it would be the best thing since we knew your fate was sealed in the harem . . . that you wouldn't be back." She reached over and squeezed my hands. "He is a kind man and works very hard. He is also a good father . . . and he's grown to love me." She looked at the birds flying from tree to tree and then continued. "And—you probably remember—Asher wants to move to Judah. He believes Jehovah is calling us there, so we are making plans with many other families to go and help in the restoration of Jerusalem."

We embraced for a long moment. Years ago, I would have been jealous to see my dream carried out in Tavita's life, but now I could rejoice with her. Suddenly, sadness began to overtake me as I realized how short our reunion would be and I would never see her again. Shaking my head to dispel those thoughts, I refused to allow my present joy to diminish. We rose and walked arm-in-arm for a long time throughout the garden, sometimes in silence, sometimes engaged in prattle about the changes in our lives, or pausing to admire the flowers.

"Queen Esther, it frightens me to think of the hardships we'll face when we leave Persia, but it's also exciting. It's almost like crossing to the Promised Land as they did long ago. We are going to the Promised Land! And Jehovah will guide us every step. We'll have to live in a tent while we build our own home, and I can't imagine how that will be, but it will surely be an adventure."

I paused before answering, almost in a whisper. "Yes, a journey to the Promised Land. I recall as a child telling Mordecai that I would journey there on a shooting star. That was so long ago."

Tavita nodded and looked off into the distance. We stopped walking, and she turned to face me. Taking my hands in hers, she said, "How about you, Esther? Are you happy?"

"Yes. I am finally content. For a while I resented being here and wondered what good could come from the sorrows in my life, but Jehovah was watching over me even when I doubted it." We began to stroll again, and I extended my hand toward the fountain at the center of the garden. "This is certainly not the life I expected, but the Lord has allowed me to serve Him at a time of great crisis, and for that I'm grateful. And He has given me a son."

A slight breeze enveloped me with the fragrance of Adonis Palestina. "It is also a comfort to have Mordecai here in the Citadel. He said that even though I am a queen, he still needs to look after me." We both laughed softly.

A servant approached us. "Pardon me, Your Majesty," he said, bowing. "King Ahasuerus wishes you to return to his side."

Tavita and I looked at each other for a long moment, and then walked, arms entwined, back to the banquet hall where we parted and rejoined our husbands.

Acknowledgments

———————

With deep appreciation to:

Professor Patricia Nestler
my first creative writing teacher

Betty Loeb
my role model and encourager

Ricki Webb
for her editing expertise and enthusiasm

The Writeen Crue
without whom I might have given up